MW01241887

C.M.SETLEDGE

SEEKING MORELS

A Short Novel

Scripture passages from the American Standard Version.
Copyright 1901 by Thomas Nelson & Sons.

Cover image from Canva.com
One Design Use License. 2022.

The characters and scenarios in this book are fictitious.
Any similarity to real persons, alive or dead, is coincidental.

An Iwinski & Setledge Imprint
First Edition
cmsetledge.com
ISBN-979-8-9865024-0-3

For Jordan and Jesse

1

DILAPIDATED stone markers crowded the corner of the small prairie. There were around two dozen of these; a closer look at the markers revealed a name and a date, the place where an otherwise forgotten body lay below.

"And what treasures do you hold down there?" a man asked. "A gold tooth, silver buttons, possibly an antique brass buckle?" The man crouched down and rubbed the edge of a gravestone. Like great slabs of bleu cheese, the stones had been burrowed by time bringing out the blue-grey rock underneath. Bits of rock crumbled at his touch, leaving a chalky residue on his fingertips. Tilted backwards, the stone façade was severely weathered. Only the last number, year of death, could be made out: 1838. "You're the last marker to be placed in this cemetery. I checked all the others. You've stood guard one hundred and fifty years."

The man straightened up and eyed the sun through gathering clouds. It was morning. Red flannel shirt sleeves were rolled up snug against his forearms. Across his shoulder hung an antique seed spreader—the kind with a leather strap, a canvas sack, and crank that spins the fan-like mechanism that scattered the seed. The three-acre prairie was good farmland, though oddly shaped, and shared a corner with gravestones.

Bidding farewell to the markers, the man left the prairie. Wooden fence posts, with barbed-wire remains rusted around them, ran along a simple country road: Moulton New Knoxville. Down the road, he approached a mailbox. The morning paper, along with a new phonebook and bills, had been stuffed inside. He pulled the paper out, issued the 1st of April, 1988. Glancing over the news, he walked up the long gravel lane that led to a farmstead.

Near the windbreak of conifers, a rustle caught his attention. "Captain, you under there?" the man called. An Australian shepherd with dull eyes poked his head out from under a pine branch near the lane.

"Listen to this headline, Cap'n," the man said to the dog, "Agricultural Crisis: Farm Mortgage Foreclosures Reach New High." The man frowned. "That's a bit on the nose for April Fool's Day don't you think?" he asked as he rolled the paper up and put it in his pants pocket. "Tell me news I don't already know," he muttered. Captain stared at him for a moment and then disappeared beneath the pines. "Alright Cap'n, I'll catch up with you later."

As he came into the farmyard, a young boy called to him, "Rain's coming, Dad!" He was playing a game of catch with an older boy under the two large catalpa trees that shaded the lawn. The lawn was the center of the farm, with the house and summer kitchen on the west side, and barns on the east side. The lane circled around the lawn and branched off to the northeast. It passed the farrowing barn and ran all the way down to the woods.

The older boy asked the man, "Are we headed to the woods or not?"

"This afternoon. Your mother and I have errands to run this morning."

"That's what I meant," continued the boy, "this afternoon."

"I left a chore list on the fridge," the man said.

He set the seed spreader on the front porch and went inside. Faux-wood paneling lined the interior walls of the entry and hallway. A small alcove to the left of the front door served as the mudroom. Beyond the alcove, a telephone was mounted on the wall. To the right was the kitchen.

"How was your walk, dear?" a woman called from the kitchen.

He entered the room, tossed the newspaper on the kitchen table, and slumped into a chair. He rubbed his face with both hands and pulled at his short, trimmed beard. "I seeded the prairie," he said to her.

She stopped what she was doing and eyed him. "Did you decide on anything?" she asked. He appeared to have not heard and picked a callous on his palm.

"Noah?" she said.

"Hmm?"

"Did you decide whether or not to sell the Wood-Mizer?"

He sat up in the chair, folding his hands neatly on the table and said, "Do you ever wonder about what's in those graves?"

She gave him a confused look.

"At the prairie," Noah said. "Those sites are well over a' hundred years old. Do you suppose they were like us?"

"Poor? German? Christian? Farmers? What do you mean?"

Noah sat back in his chair, sighing. "Yes, poor German Christian farmers."

"What made you think of that?"

"I don't know," Noah said, waving the matter aside, "and I haven't decided whether to part with Dad's sawmill."

She rubbed his shoulder. "We'll figure it out," she said, rubbing a little harder, "won't we?"

Noah nodded.

9

She added, "And you should tell Jonah if we decide to sell the Wood-Mizer." There was a pause and more shoulder rubbing, "Right?"

"Yes, Eleanor, yes," he said.

"I'm going to get ready. Coffee's on the counter," Eleanor said, leaving the room.

While Noah poured a mug of coffee, the boys came in. "What time is service tonight?" the younger son asked.

"Seven," Noah answered, resuming his seat at the table.

"I told you, Jonah! Today's Good Friday."

"Yeah, whatever." Jonah went to the fridge and released a slip of paper from a magnet. After looking at it, he said, "Dad, I think it's gonna' rain today."

"It's not forecasted to rain till tonight. Just ask your grandma," Noah said.

"But if it does, do you still want us to attach the loader and hitch the wagon?" Jonah said, pointing to the task on the slip of paper.

"Are you and Reinhardt able to do that on your own?" Noah asked.

"Of course!" Jonah said.

Noah took a long drink of coffee, then turned to look out the window which overlooked the porch. He could see the clouds gathering in the sky. Jonah stuffed the list in the pocket of his flannel and took a seat at the table. Dark blue eyes roamed the table's surface, his young hands—already rough with signs of labor—began to fidget with the edge of the morning newspaper. The father and son sitting at the table looked like the same people: one just younger, smaller, and less hairy than the other.

"Dad, remember how I wanted to make some money?"

"Yes, a worthy endeavor."

"What about sawing wood? I know that's not something you would do, but I could."

"If that's something you wanted to do when you are older, that's fine with me."

Jonah scooted the newspaper around on the kitchen table. "Yeah, that's the problem. I'm not old enough yet, but if I had a mo-ped…"

"At the moment neither of us could buy a mo-ped. You could find work at a nearby farm; you could ride your bicycle. Then you can save up for a mo-ped, or keep saving until you're sixteen and buy a car. That's what I would do. And the Wood-Mizer may not—"

"Noah, have you seen my umbrella?" His wife called from another room.

"It's not going to rain today, Ella."

She came into the kitchen. "Thanks, dear, but that doesn't help me find it. I don't feel completely comfortable with the idea of a mo-ped, Jonah." She went to the counter and prepped a coffee to go. "Did you already get a cup?"

"Yeah," Noah said. "No worries, Ella. Jonah can save up for a car." He gave a confirming nod to Jonah.

"Really?" She looked to Jonah, a smile and sigh escaped her. "Two more years. Why are you boys growing up so fast?" She came to Jonah and gave him a squeeze around his shoulders from where he sat in the chair.

"Less than two years, Mom," Jonah corrected.

She just smiled. "Noah, are we all set?"

"Minus an umbrella, we're good to go," he said, standing up to leave. "Jonah," he turned his attention back to his son, "if it starts raining, don't worry about the loader and wagon."

"I think it's gonna' rain," Jonah said.

***

Creamy white and buttery yellow, the colors of Noah's 76' Chevy C30—with just a little rust—faded down the road. After watching the truck leave, the two boys set to work on the morning chores. First, they tended to the new litters of Berkshires: "Hey Reinhardt, rock, paper, scissors; loser spreads bedding," Jonah said. Reinhardt's *scissors* lost to Jonah's *rock*.

"Best two out of three?" Reinhardt asked.

"Hmm, not today."

Next, they fed the Barred Rocks and Black Giants. Collecting the eggs, they took them to Grandma in the summer kitchen. Grandma made the boys "Eggs in a Basket," and they asked her about the weather.

"It'll rain, but later tonight," she said.

After finishing their second breakfast, they thanked Grandma and went outside—their morning mostly spent.

"Okay Reinhardt, I've been stalling," Jonah said, "We've only one thing left on the list, and I saved the most difficult thing for last." Jonah led his younger brother to the shed.

One end of the shed roof was sagging, but it had endured enough winter storms, wind, hail, freezing rain, and sleet to give everyone confidence it would continue to stand until the end of time. Housed underneath was a genuine circus wagon.

Years ago, their granddad had purchased it at an auction, "They had absolutely no idea what they were selling!" He exclaimed, "I got it for pennies on the dollar." Painted in forest green with golden trim, it was one of the prettiest pieces of farm equipment. Next to the wagon was the less lovely Ford 861 tractor. Though originally painted in burnt orange with tan accents, decades of rust and touchups left the tractor looking dumpy.

"Do we need the loader at all?" Reinhardt asked.

"Don't you listen *at all?*"

"Uh, sorry I forgot."

Jonah climbed into the pilot seat. He labored the clutch down with his left foot, right foot on the brake pedals, pulled the choke all the way, and turned the key. The tractor cranked to life.

Hitching the wagon took several attempts. They had to back the tractor up close enough to leverage the wagon tongue into alignment with the hitch. Reinhardt held the tongue up and complained, "Jonah, this is getting pretty heavy." He had to yell over the rattle of the tractor.

"Will you calm down? I've almost got it." And eventually he did, and the wagon was hitched.

"Crap," Jonah said once he pulled the wagon out and around the side of the shed.

"What?"

"We should have connected the loader first, then the wagon."

Reinhardt whistled a low note.

"As if you had any idea." Jonah rolled his eyes. "Just help me line the bracket up." Aligning the tractor bracket and loader required precision and strength. Jonah failed to be precise with the tractor. He climbed down and tested his strength by trying to shove the loader into position.

"Why don't we just unhitch the wagon?" Reinhardt asked.

"Because you suck at helping. I'm not doing that over again." Jonah continued pushing on the loader attachment. Reinhardt stood still. "Are you going to help me or what?"

"I just don't like when you're being mean."

"Really, Reiner? Or should I say Whiner? You're such a weakling."

"Right there!"

"What!?"

"You're doing it again, calling me a whiner, saying I'm a lousy helper. Don't take your frustrations out on me."

"Oh, you think I'm taking my frustrations out? This is what that looks like." He punched Reinhardt in the arm. Reinhardt started to tear up. "See?" said Jonah, "Weakling." Reinhardt turned without another word and marched off. "I don't need your help!" Jonah yelled. "Better off without you."

***

The old "Diamond Savings and Loan" name could still be seen outside the "Home Savings Bank's" doors. Two men— one in a suit and tie and the other in a denim uniform speckled with paint—argued about the old letters' visibility.

"It's all really too bad," Noah said when they walked in. "That painter didn't want to see Diamond's go either." They sat in front of a new desk, much broader than the one before the bank's recent acquisition. A glossy name plaque read "Mr. Don Schreiber."

"I really don't like this 'Mr. Schreiber's' desk," Noah said.

"I definitely don't like seeing it twice in one week," Eleanor said.

The new banker walked down the hall. In front of a hallway mirror he paused to tighten his loose neck tie and practice a smile. He entered the office bringing the smell of Stetson cologne with him. At the desk, he folded his hands and wore his rehearsed smile.

"Good morning, Mr. and Mrs...." the banker glanced at papers on his desk, "Brandtmeyer. I've looked over the promissory note." He spread his hands over the papers. "It was this kind of, er, partnering Diamond Savings and Loan was loved for, but look at them now." He held his hands up like a magician revealing that the card had disappeared. His smile vanished also. He furrowed his brow and said, "The unfortunate truth is, it's been ninety days and there can be no further extensions." With face muscles strained, he continued, "I'm sorry to say this, Mr. Brandtmeyer, but this is the last month before we're forced to... to pursue our legal remedies."

Noah breathed deep and leaned back in his chair. His wife at his side gripped his hand. "I have a little cash coming my way soon. I can keep up on the payments; it's just taking a bit of time. I wanted to ask if we could renegotiate monthly payments or—with a little freed up cash—refinance for a better interest rate."

"Options, yes. Interest rates continue to be abysmal, but better than your current one. If you have the money to refinance," the man leaned forward in his chair, "and we make some other adjustments I've previously alluded to, we can reduce the monthly payment. But, Mr. Brandtmeyer, with respect, in your situation, will you honestly be able to make even a reduced monthly payment?"

"Depends on how reduced." Noah's gaze had fallen at the mention of *other adjustments previously alluded to.*

The man behind the desk looked down at his papers, began to frame a word in his mouth, reconsidered, cleared his throat and then said, "A credit life insurance policy on a loan can be dropped at any time. By dropping your father's credit life insurance, the payment—"

"I don't want to go over all that again," Noah interrupted, rubbing his temples with his fingers. Eleanor placed her hand on his thigh and stared at the floor. The combination of Xerox, warm printed paper, Stetson's cologne and fresh paint in the air were beginning to make her eyes red and watery.

"Options, Mr. and Mrs. Brandtmeyer. That, along with a new interest rate would represent a considerable decrease in the monthly payment. So sorry to bring up a sensitive point, but in this case, it bears directly on the matter at hand." he cleared his throat again and pulled at his neck tie, "Is there any hope of finding your father?" Then he lowered his voice, "Or if he is indeed deceased?"

"I'll be able to make another few months' payments starting soon," Noah said firmly. "If I can't make the payments, what am I up against, what do I need to know?"

The banker loosened his neck tie. He sat up straight and said, "Unfortunately, Mr. Brandtmeyer, the only remaining remedy to us is repossession: the house, barns, machinery, woodlands, even the crops planted in the fields. In a word: Foreclosure." He exhaled and folded his hands together. "I'm very glad to hear about your coming windfall, but the bank's position is very clear."

"Yes," Noah said, "and to be clear, the credit life insurance policy remains. You said thirty days for the first payment? I'll have it next week, take that in good faith." Noah stood up. "Come on Eleanor, we have all we need to know. Good day, Mr. Schreiber. I'll have a check here next week."

They didn't wait to hear Mr. Schreiber make any parting farewells. Once in the parking lot Eleanor asked, "So, going into that I didn't know we had one-hundred percent decided to sell your father's Wood-Mizer?"

"What a tax collector, what an unrepentant tax collecting..." Noah's rant stalled out. "Sorry Eleanor, what did you say?" She repeated herself and Noah said, "I wasn't sure going into it, but realistically, do you see any other options?"

She looked down. "Can't the bank just understand and make the extension?" She was choking up, "Can't the credit life insurance agency advance us money?"

Noah opened the door to the cab, "I can't change the fine print. I can't make Dad reappear, dead or alive! What do you want me to do? Hire a lawyer? Pay him with bacon?"

She slumped into the passenger seat; her head fell into her hands. "It's just so unfair!" and she began to cry.

Noah put his hand on Eleanor. For a few minutes Noah stayed like that, leaning against the truck with his hand on Eleanor as they mellowed. She blew her nose into a handkerchief and sat limp in the passenger's seat like a deflated air bag.

The sun shone through a small part in the clouds. The town was dry; it had not rained as of yet. Saint Marys' Main Street was lined with brick stores, each sharing a wall with its neighbors.

"Let's walk down the street," Noah offered.

An old canal separated a section of the stores' masonry, and a bridge spanned the waterway. Standing on the bridge gave them a beautiful view of the town park: full of grass, trees, and park benches. There was also a historical replica canal boat in the water accompanied by a plaster donkey standing on the tow path. Next to the donkey was a large plaque which read: Miami & Erie Canal. A wrought iron stairway attached to the bridge gave pedestrians access to the park grounds.

"I'd like to head down to the park," Eleanor said. The sun and fresh air had brought her relief.

"Okay, I have some interest in that store up ahead," Noah pointed across the bridge. "I'll meet you in the park in a few?"

The storefront had panoramic windows spanning their front wall. A three-dimensional sign supported a steam engine that looked like it was coming out of the building. 'Traders Co.' was written in large red letters. Noah entered the store. Floor to ceiling were shelves cluttered with secondhand goods and novelties seemingly arranged by a tornado. A woman worked the cash register and behind her a young boy sat on the floor building a LEGO set.

Noah approached the woman at the cash register. "Do you buy as well as sell?"

"Can I see your I.D.?" She asked, "It's policy."

"Sure," Noah gave the woman his driver's license.

"One moment, please."

Behind her was a stairway descending down. Across the entrance was a rope with a sign attached reading "No Admittance." She stepped over the rope and descended, taking Noah's license with her. He tapped his fingers on the glass countertop. Inside were old trinkets: silver spoons, tarnished broaches, pendants, and rings. He looked at these for a minute; then to a clock mounted behind the cash register. Another minute passed. The rustling of LEGO's drew Noah's attention to the small boy.

"Is that a pirate set?" Noah asked.

The boy darted a shy glance at Noah.

"I have a young son who would like that," Noah said.

The child smiled and held up a knight minifigure, "It's my Black Falcon's Fortress." Noah smiled back at him.

The woman returned up the stairs. "Al will see you." She gave Noah his license and pointed down the stairs. Noah came around the counter, eyeing the dark stairwell, and then the woman. "You can step over it." She waved him on.

Moth balls and cigarettes scented the basement. Table upon table filled the floor space. By the light from the stairway, Noah could see boxes filled with indexed coins from various nations and ages.

Across the room was a small office space. The door was open and an old man was sitting inside. He had thick-rimmed glasses and wore a tweed jacket. As he smoked a cigarette, he worked on a model train by the light of a green-shaded lamp. Mounted on the wall behind him a long metal apparatus hung.

Looking up from his work, the man motioned for Noah to come.

"Guten tag, Mr. Brandtmeyer," the man said. He ground the butt of his cigarette in an ashtray and reached to give Noah a firm handshake.

"You can call me Al. Please, take a seat." Al resumed his work on the model train. Tiny bits littered the desk. He attached a little piece of railing to a train car. "Do you like trains, Mr. Brandtmeyer?"

"Sure."

"I love trains. I used to operate them in the old country."

"You have a lovely sign of one out front," Noah said.

"Danke schön."

Noah was eyeing the item mounted on the wall. Now that he was closer, he saw it was some sort of military weapon similar to a Bazooka.

Al looked up from his work with a smile. "You like my Panzerfäust, yaw?"

"Huh?"

He pointed to the item mounted above him, "Panzerfäust. All the goot little boys trained with them in the old country. Do you know these things?"

"My ancestors immigrated in the eighteen hundred's."

"Ah, goot. Goot." Al frowned. He resumed his work on the model train. "Though others would say it's a shame. Sprechen sie Deutsch?"

"No."

"No hard feelings. What do you do for a living?"

"Farm."

"How is that going for you?"

"Been better."

Al's hands hovered over the miniature train construction. "Das leben ist kein Ponyhof[1]," he said then looked up from his work, "Sorry to hear that Mr. Brandtmeyer. My daughter tells me you have items for sale?"

"Heirlooms: bits and pieces of gold, silver buttons, antiquities and the like."

"I see no parcels." Al held his hands open as if ready to receive the heirlooms.

"Oh sorry, it was more speculative. I didn't even know if selling was possible here."

"You have not brought them?"

"Not with me, no."

"We hold a 'Traders Fair' last Thursday of the month, just had one yesterday." Al pointed out the office window. "You saw those boxes coming in, with the coins? That's part of the trading guild. Best time to sell your wares."

Noah shuffled and shook his head. "Sorry, that won't do." He swallowed a lump building in his throat, "I can't wait till the end of the month."

"You need cash now?"

Noah nodded.

Al leaned back in his chair. From a pocket inside his jacket, he brought out a pack of cigarettes. "Cigarette? Imported from the Fatherland." He held the pack out. Noah declined. Al lit up and took a long contemplative draw.

"How interesting, Mr. Brandtmeyer burnt on farming. Is it a big farm?"

"No."

"Just down old 33, South of Moulton?"

"Uh, yes." Noah frowned.

---

[1] The life isn't a pony farm.

"Don't look so incredulous, Mr. Brandtmeyer. My daughter showed me your license."

"Oh, right." Noah glanced at the Panzerfäust, the model train, a filing cabinet in the corner, and the smoke curling around the green lampshade. His hands were getting clammy.

Al continued thinking on his cigarette. He opened the desk drawer and brought out a belt buckle. "Gott mit uns[2]." Al said holding the buckle up offering Noah a full view of the relic; the words Al had spoken were written within an embossed circle above an eagle perched on a swastika. "You look displeased, Mr. Brandtmeyer. You are not the first man to offer me heirlooms."

"Oh, right of course."

"Pieces from this era fetch high prices. Are your heirlooms such as these?"

"Uh, no."

Al winked and returned the belt buckle to the drawer. "I want to help you, Mr. Brandtmeyer. I like you. But truthfully, I don't have cash on hand myself."

He rose from his seat and went to the filing cabinet in the corner of the room. From a ring of keys on his belt, Al unlocked the filing cabinet and fingered through the manila folders. After a minute he closed the filling drawer and re-locked it. "How many years have you been farming? You've got strong right hand, calloused. Let me see them."

"My hands?" Noah questioned.

"Please, raise them."

Noah proffered his hands. Al eyed them.

"I have it," Al beamed. The green light of the lamp reflected off his glasses. "I'll hold your wares as collateral and I'll hire

---

[2] God with us.

you, just to make a delivery. Once the job is done, I share profits with you, yaw?"

"I would need to know more about the job."

"It's a goot job, requires strength," he slapped Noah's shoulders, "which you have, yet also sensitivity and wisdom." He pointed to Noah's head. "And I can tell you have that too. You are perfect for the job. Allow me to check my dates. And make a few phone calls. I will send you a message soon. The job would be completed by the end of next week; can you wait that long for cash in hand?"

"Would it be in hand by Friday?"

"Of course," Al smiled and waved his cigarette.

"Okay," Noah said.

"Wunderbar, Mr. Brandtmeyer. This may be the beginnings of a great partnership."

"Do you want my phone number to reach me?"

"No need." Al wore a wry smile and extended his right hand. Noah shook it. "Auf wiedersehen, Mr. Brandtmeyer."

Noah climbed back up the stairs, hands burrowed deep in his pockets and lines furrowed deeper still on his forehead. "What am I doing?" he muttered to himself.

He lost himself in a maze of cluttered shelves, when, nestled between wicker-baskets and picture frames, a lantern caught his eye. The lantern was quite small. And the clever shutter mechanism appealed to Noah; the light could be narrowed or fanned by turning a knob. He bought it, and before finding his wife in the park, he stashed his purchase under the seat in his truck.

2

REINHARDT was sitting on the porch swing when the parents returned home.

"How'd the morning go?" Noah asked.

Reinhardt shrugged, "Typical morning, I guess."

"Is the fence work prepped?"

Reinhardt slipped off the swing and shook his head, "We didn't get that far."

"Where is your older brother?"

"I think he must have gone to the woods, or the Quonset, I saw him walking that way earlier."

"Did you have lunch?"

"Eggs in a Basket." He smiled.

"Reinhardt and I are going to head out to the woods," Noah said to Eleanor, "if you see Jonah, send him out there please." In the mud room, he grabbed the chainsaw and a can of gasoline mix. They went to the shed where the tractor and wagon sat jackknifed and loader arm still detached. Noah set the chainsaw and gas into the loader bucket.

"Close but no cigar, huh?" He put both hands on the loader and gave it a push; it budged an inch. "Order of operations," he said smiling, "I'll have to teach you and Jonah that."

He started the tractor and maneuvered it enough to release pressure on the hitch pin. "Reinhardt, pop the hitch pin please," he called over the gentle engine rumble. With the movement unhindered, Noah lined the tractor up and clamped the loader quickly. "Practice makes perfect, not really, but it definitely improves efficiency. Why don't you hop into the seat and back it up."

Reinhardt's face grimaced.

"Practice also builds confidence."

"Alright then," Reinhardt said and climbed into position.

"Just put it in first gear—reverse obviously," Noah instructed, he took a step back.

Reinhardt fumbled with the levers to engage the gears.

"Just keep it all at an idle, foot off the brake, easy off the clutch."

The tractor jolted into reverse as the clutch forced Reinhardt's youthful foot into submission.

"Easy there, turn your wheels, that's close enough. Now brake."

Reinhardt strained the clutch back down with his left leg, and struggled to pushed the right and left brake pedals with his right foot. The little tractor slowed to a shaky halt. "Pop it into neutral," Noah instructed.

He lifted the wagon tongue and the hitch was close enough that he could rock the wagon the rest of the way. Reinhardt watched his dad work the wagon into place and drop the hitch pin through the holes. "Practice builds strength too." Noah smiled.

Noah took the driver's seat, and Reinhardt rode on the hitch. As they rounded the farrowing barn, Noah stopped to check the rain gauge mounted on the corner fence post. There was water in the gauge.

"Did it rain?" Noah asked.

"I don't think so."

Noah frowned at the rain gauge and rubbed his beard. "Reinhardt, hop down. I want to show you something."

Together they walked back to the farmhouse. Noah opened the storm hatch to the basement. They both descended the smooth cement steps. Cobwebs hung in tatters from either side; the opening of the hatch caused daddy-long-legs to scatter.

From a shelf, Noah gave Reinhardt a Mason jar. "Open this please and grab three of those little packets." The packets were about the size of a standard Band-Aid with a color scale ranging from green to orange with a number system corresponding to each color.

"What are these?"

"Test strips," Noah replied. "Come along. I'll show you."

They left the basement and went to the garden side of the home. Along the wall, there sat a large barrel that collected rain water from a crack in the rain gutter from above.

"Open one of the packets and dip a test strip in the barrel."

Reinhardt dipped the strip and watched as a color emerged on the tip: green. He looked at the packet's number that correlated with the color. "Green means zero," he said, holding up the test strip.

"That means zero hardness: no calcium, magnesium, or iron. Rain water is naturally soft. Let's go back to the farrowing barn." Noah had Reinhardt repeat the process, testing water from the hydrant near the farrowing barn.

Reinhardt watched a burnt orange hue emerge that matched the "15" range.

"The barnyard has well water. Well water is full of minerals collected as water seeps into the ground—in this case 15 grains per gallon. We call that hard water."

"Hand me the last test strip," Noah said as he detached the rain gauge. He tipped it sideways and the strip touched the water. As the color appeared, he held it out for Reinhardt to see. "Is this water in the gauge hard or soft?"

"Hard."

***

At the wood's northwest corner was a Quonset. The inexpensive corrugated steel shed looked like a giant tin can cut in half and tipped on its side. Inside was the LT-40 Wood-Mizer, a portable monorail sawmill. Noah and Reinhardt found Jonah sitting in the operator's chair of the sawmill reading a small book.

"Did it rain?" asked Noah.

"Just a little," Jonah said, not looking up from his reading.

"Is that one of Granddad's journals?"

Jonah nodded. "I'll put it back," he said and walked through a door at the back of the Quonset. A partition separated the bay from a shop office. Through the doorway, a desk and bookshelf could be seen. When he returned, he said, "I was reading in his journal about the fence line along the woods."

"Help Reinhardt put this stack of boards on the wagon," Noah said, pointing out a pile of lumber among several small piles. "What year was that?"

"1982."

Noah nodded his head. "I remember that year." He took a chain and log tongs off a shelf against the partitioning wall.

"What happened in '82?" Reinhardt asked as they loaded the boards.

"That's the year your granddad bought a Wood-Mizer." Noah said. He set tools and hardware into the tractor's loader bucket. "It was a smaller model then, LT-30. Later he upgraded to this model." Noah patted the operator's box on the LT-40.

"Anyways…" he trailed off in thought, mounted the tractor and settled into the seat, "all aboard."

They crept down a path along the edge of the woods. Bare trees stood like numerous pillars, naked limbs reaching skyward. Sunlight flooded the woodland floor, and the ground sprouted with green. Soon the whole woodland would be vibrant with life. Between them and the woods was a fence line, with an occasional gate opening to paths that went deep into the woods. They stopped at the first gate.

"This looks even more smashed up than before," Jonah said. They all dismounted the tractor and stood looking at a fallen cedar, which had crushed the gate.

"Now that the snow's melted, you can see everything clearly enough," Noah said as he wrested a broken piece of wood from the gate. "The hinges we can salvage.

"When your granddad bought the Wood-Mizer and I was planning to raise a heritage breed with acorn finishing, we joined forces on this project here. That was all in '82. Dad cut his teeth on the trees from these woods. He cut all the planks for the stretches of fence you see all around here."

"Why don't we ever use it now?" Reinhardt asked.

"He cut so much wood, we're set for life. The boards you just loaded were from '82."

"But I'd like to get back into it," Jonah said. "I remember going with Granddad to jobsites. We'd spend the whole day sawing huge tree trunks into boards."

"I'm glad that you did that with him. It was always your granddad's passion. He had a sizeable operation milling wood— good cash flow." Noah waved his hand as if to wave off the thought and shook his head. "Unfortunately, it wasn't the job for me, cutting lumber for someone else—away from the farm all day, animals needing fed. And honestly when you're doing those jobs, the ones that pay anything to make it worth your while, you sit in the operator's chair all day." He shook his head again, "But your granddad, now he had a knack for it.

"Jonah, unhitch the wagon." Noah grabbed the chainsaw from the loader bucket. After a few good tugs, it roared to life and the fumes filled the air. Its teeth chewed through an arm of the tree, spewing mealy woodchips to the ground. Once sectioned, the chainsaw quieted to an idle.

"Jonah, fasten the chain and skidding tongs to the bucket— good, now lift the loader over the branch." Jonah moved the tractor into position. Noah caught the tongs on the wood and gave the signal. Jonah dragged the piece off to the side.

"Reinhardt, start collecting up the free boards into a pile," Noah said.

Within the hour, they had the tree quartered and piled to the side, and Reinhardt had piled the broken boards alongside the wagon.

"What a mess one tree makes," Reinhardt said.

"Looks like this one should have been removed in '82, Dad."

"Suppose so, but then we wouldn't have this fun project to work on together."

"Loads of fun."

"Do you boys want to run the chainsaw a little?"

"No," said Reinhardt, "I don't want to lose a finger."

"I'd like to," Jonah said, "to run the chainsaw, I mean—not lose a finger."

"Can I look around for morels in the meantime?" Reinhardt asked.

"It's probably too early in the season, but okay. The sinkhole isn't too far to the northeast of here," Noah pointed. "That's usually a good spot, but be back in about fifteen." Then Noah turned to Jonah and began his chainsaw instruction.

Reinhardt walked along the sinkhole's boundary. Evidence of a shift in the ground was visible, though time had eroded the sharp edge. Water had eroded paths between trunk and roots, like tiny canyons the width of a hand. The ground sloped, like a shallow funnel, towards the center where the last of the snowmelt soaked into the ground. Reinhardt gave a shiver as he looked at the dark water in the center, and then he began inspecting the dank areas: drifts of decaying leaves, rotting tree trunks, and slabs of fallen bark.

Jonah sawed through the cedar. Despite the strong chainsaw fumes of gas and oil, the distinct aroma of the tree filled the air. Its sweet smell coated his boots in the form of little wood schnibbles. While cutting a section of trunk, the chainsaw sputtered and died.

"Outta' gas, Dad."

Over by the loader, Noah poured the gas and oil mixture into the chainsaw.

He asked Jonah, "Have I shown you how to mix the chainsaw gas?"

"Granddad showed me. Forty parts gas, one part oil."

Noah nodded. He finished and capped the tank. Through the trees, he saw Reinhardt wandering in search of mushrooms. Noah took a deep breath and sighed. "It's a beautiful season, plants sprouting, Redbud blooming early, spring pigs being born, longer days, warm breezes…"

Jonah stood next to him listening and nodding his head.

Noah turned to his son; his steady gaze focused Jonah's attention, "Why did you lie about the rain today?"

"What?" Jonah asked.

"I know you put water in the gauge."

"Did Reinhardt see? Did he rat on me?"

"No, your brother had no idea. Why did you do it?"

Jonah began scraping at the bits of wood stuck on one of his boots with the other. "Sometimes we have a lot of stuff to do around the farm, and Reinhardt just isn't all that helpful. Today we were trying to hook up the wagon and loader and I'm trying to do all this stuff and he's just getting whiny to the point I can't work with him." He shook his head. Noah continued to watch him. The silence forced Jonah to continue, "Reinhardt walked off and I couldn't finish the work alone."

"So you lied to excuse your unfinished work?"

Jonah kept scraping at the wood bits on his boot. "I punched Reinhardt—just in the arm."

"I see. Do you want me to punch you?"

Jonah took a quick step back, looking alert at his dad.

"Just in the arm," Noah said.

Jonah shook his head.

"Reinhardt's eleven. You can't expect him to do as much as you. Have some patience. You should have been honest and asked for help. Am I understood?"

Jonah nodded.

They heard Reinhardt tromping towards them.

"Apologize to your little brother," his dad finished with a stern look.

Reinhardt returned and looked at the two of them. "I didn't hear the chainsaw anymore, so I'm back. I didn't find any morels." He shrugged. "Too early."

"I figured as much," said Noah.

"Dad, how'd the sinkhole get there?" Reinhardt asked

"Sometimes, when you have underground water, erosion can make the ground above collapse."

"But just right here?"

"What do you mean?"

"What stops everything from just collapsing everywhere?"

"It's just here where water drains into an underground aquifer or stream. I can't explain it exactly. Years ago, I think when your granddad first bought the land, a geologist explained some of that." He finished with a loud clearing of his throat and leaned into Jonah.

"Sorry for earlier," Jonah said looking at his brother.

Reinhardt looked down at his empty hands. "No mushrooms," he said quietly and rubbed his eyes.

Noah gave Jonah a guiding push forward. The brothers stood facing one another. Jonah extended his hand and Reinhardt shook it.

"And sorry I was the way I was," Reinhardt said.

"It's okay, and we can look for morels again in another day or two."

Reinhardt smiled.

"Can't you guys give each other a hug?" Noah asked.

Jonah did a quick one arm back-pat while Reinhardt gave him a solid two arm embrace.

"Now the two of you load these logs neatly on the wagon."

Then Noah fired up the chainsaw and went back to work.

***

The bare trees began to cast long shadows when Noah and the boys finished mounting the repaired gate. With logs loaded and tools collected, the tractor puttered along the woods and drew up to the backside of the Quonset. A door in the center of the arched wall opened directly into Granddad's old shop office. Two large windows were set on either side of the door. The lowering sunlight cut through the panes illuminating dusty brown bottles sitting on the window sill.

"Let's put the tools back through here," Noah said. They each grabbed an armful of tools from the loader. Through the back door, they passed through the shop office following a path made between old chicken crates and boxes.

"Dad, I had a question about Granddad's journals," Jonah asked after setting down his load. They all went back into Granddad's office. Jonah paused at the bookshelf. "I've read them all." He touched the journals. Each one had a year written in gold on its blue binding. "What month of '86 did he disappear?"

"May."

"There isn't a journal for that year on the shelf, but he definitely would have had one, right?"

"I remember looking for a journal, but none of us could find one. When he went missing, a few of his things disappeared with him. I assumed the journal was one of those things."

"What else was missing?"

"His compass, wrist watch, canteen and pack, basic things you would take on a short hike. Your grandma might remember specifics. The police 'deduced' that there wasn't any indication he meant to go on a long journey."

"So, you think the journal is with him?"

"I do," Noah confirmed.

"I always thought he just disappeared from his bed," Reinhardt commented.

"No, not at all, he definitely went out and didn't intend to go far. He didn't take his wallet with him for instance."

"If he didn't vanish like a ghost, but never came back, where is he?" Jonah questioned.

"And that's the million-dollar question... well, a hundred-thousand-dollar one. Either he was carried off by a large wild animal that isn't native to these parts," he counted on his fingers, "and that really doesn't seem plausible, or he was abducted—"

"Like by aliens!?" blurted Reinhardt.

"No, that seems even more unlikely than wild animals," but he counted it off on his fingers anyways, "abducted, taken, kidnapped."

"Grand-napped?"

Noah continued, "Also not likely, usually there's a ransom to follow and it helps to ransom someone from wealth, so double nix there." He held three fingers; the little finger remained. The boys looked at it in anticipation.

"And the last possibility?" Jonah asked. Both the boys' eyes were wide and waiting.

"Right, the last possibility and going theory—and this is the position held by the credit life insurance agency—is that he ran off, probably living in the Bahamas somewhere."

"What!? Well, that's stupid!" said Jonah.

"Aliens are more likely!" said Reinhardt.

"It's the most 'justifiable theory' given the current evidence, according to the agency's denial letter."

"But what do you think, Dad?" Jonah asked.

"Listen boys, I'd like to hope Grandad's alright, but I don't have enough fingers to count the possibilities on. I don't know. I may never know and that's the worst of it." He turned to look through the window. "We're probably waiting out our seven years to receive the Death Claim, and be left with nothing to show for it."

"We have plenty to show for it," Jonah said.

"Right," Noah whispered as he continued looking out the window. He blew his nose in his handkerchief. A moment of silence passed. The younger brother moved a cardboard filing box off the old couch. Dust flecks stirred in the shaft of light, and he sneezed. "It's sort of a mess in here," he said, wiping his nose with a flannel sleeve. Cautiously, he sat on the tattered cushions.

33

Jonah fetched a journal from the shelf. He made room for himself at the desk. Opening the journal, his fingers flipped to a favorite entry.

"Fine birthday, quite copacetic. Marilla at her best as usual..." Jonah skimmed a few lines, "received from Noah, Eleanor and the boys a handsome Bulova self-winding wrist watch." Beaming, he asked, "Was that the watch he took, Dad?"

Their father stirred. "Hmm, what was that son?" Half turning his head towards where Jonah sat, then looking back out the window he nodded. "Yes, Bulova watch, I believe so." He gave a strong blow of his nose into the handkerchief and it sounded soggy.

***

Noah and the boys drove the tractor and wagon into the barnyard. From the farmhouse the dinner bell rang. Eleanor leaned out the front door and shouted, "I saw you driving up, dinner's been ready!"

Grandma walked out of the summer kitchen carrying a dish across the lawn and into the house. Eleanor held the door for her. "And now dessert is ready too!" she added.

They waved to the ladies. "We'll be right up!" Noah called. "Will you boys check on the pigs?"

Jonah and Reinhardt dismounted.

"Dad, what's copacetic?" asked Reinhardt.

"Hurry along. Ask your mother to add it to your vocab list."

Reinhardt rolled his eyes. "Ah, come on."

Noah smiled and chuckled. "It's been a copacetic afternoon with the two of you. I can tell you that. Quickly, you don't want to keep your mother waiting." He drove the tractor and wagon around to the backside of the farmhouse and unhitched the old green circus wagon by the wood hatch. Then he parked the tractor in the shed and went in for dinner.

A few minutes later the boys came in. They tugged their boots off in the mudroom. Bits of wood and straw littered the ground. They could hear their parents and Grandma talking at the dining room table.

"It makes me no difference, as I've said, but I can only speak for myself," Grandma said. "Now if it means living here, or moving into town, that's a no brainer. Why did you sit on it for so long?"

"Mom—" Noah began, but he was cut off by both boys running in.

"Moving into town, Grandma!?" they both exclaimed.

There was an awkward stutter from both Noah and Grandma. Eleanor spoke up, "Grandma's not moving away from us boys, settle down. Did you wash up? Go wash up before your food is cold."

"I didn't even hear them come in. Did you?" Noah asked under his breath. The others shook their heads.

Noah listened for a moment. The boys were washing in the hallway bathroom. "In short, I've been sitting on everything for two years with the hope that Dad would show up. But we can't wait another five to receive the Death Claim for the credit life insurance." The water in the hallway bathroom stopped running. "Let's table it for now."

They all nodded in agreement.

When the boys returned to the table, Noah was quick to ask a blessing for the food: "Lord, thank you for this day, and for the food. Please give us wisdom; help us to be content in all circumstances and trust in You. In Jesus' name, amen."

"Amen," the family said, and before either son could get in a word, Noah continued, "Reinhardt officially made the first search for morels this year."

"Ah!" Grandma exclaimed. "But you didn't find any, did you?"

Reinhardt shook his head.

"Keep it up; it's already turning out to be a warm spring."

***

By the time they finished dinner, the sun had set. It was only 6:40, the last weekend before time would "spring ahead" in the wee hours of Sunday morning. But on this first day of April, it was a fitting dark and stormy Good Friday.

The Brandtmeyers made the short two-mile drive into the small village of New Knoxville. They arrived in time for the church bells to strike seven. The sky finally broke and the rain began to fall as they entered the church doors. They climbed the stairs to the balcony. The pastor, middle-aged, but with a touch of grey in his hair, was already in the pulpit.

He had begun the reading from Matthew, "…there was darkness over all the land…"

"Shh," Eleanor whispered to her boys as they bumped about taking their seats in a pew.

The reading continued, "My God, my God, why hast thou forsaken me?"

"I'm feeling a little 'forsaken' myself, if you know what I mean," Noah whispered as he took his seat next to his wife.

"Shh." Eleanor nudged her husband.

"Sorry, been a long day, my mind's still racing," Noah whispered back.

Eleanor put her hand on Noah's thigh. "It'll all work out somehow," she whispered, "but please, I'm trying to listen."

"…filled it with vinegar, and put it on a reed, and gave him to drink…"

"I can't focus, Ella. What if Dad is alive somewhere and really has forsaken us?"

"I know how it's gnawing at you. I loved your father too." She reached in her purse for a tissue and offered it to her husband, "but please, listen."

Noah waved off the offered tissue. "I'm fine, thanks."

"…And Jesus cried again with a loud voice, and yielded up his spirit…"

"Maybe I should speak with Pastor John about it, again."

"That's a good idea," Eleanor whispered back.

"I will. Sunday."

Eleanor patted Noah's thigh.

"…The earth did quake; and the rocks were rent; and the tombs were opened…"

Under Eleanor's hand she could feel Noah suddenly begin to tremble. She eyed him with uneasiness and offered her tissue again. Noah shook his head; there was a tremor in his whisper, "I'll be okay. I was just listening to Pastor John."

3

THE AUSTRALIAN shepherd rested under the conifers. During the winter, he spent his time under the porch. As spring marched across the landscape, he settled under the windbreak, which lined the west side of the farm. Under the trees, a perpetual cycle of fresh pine needles kept the dog's hovel dry and comfortable. From this vantage, he observed the days. He could see down the lane to Moulton New Knoxville Road. Languid brown eyes watched the Saturday morning traffic. The spring view and the sporting it provided was good: a tractor and planter chugged down the road before dawn, several trucks loaded with seed bags sped by, and a black LeBaron convertible unexpectedly turned off the road and crept up the lane. Ears pulled the rest of his head, neck, and body up into sentinel position. He barked and charged the car. The car continued its slow creep, and the dog jogged beside it.

The man was ducking behind the car door. He remained there until Noah came from the shed. "That'll do, Cap'n." Captain retreated to the porch steps.

Eleanor came out and pet him on the head. "I haven't seen you in a while," she said.

"Good morning, Sir. The name's Ed," said the man as he exited the convertible. He wore a neat black suit and tie. Extending his hand, he continued, "Is this Brandtmeyer Farms?"

"Depends," Noah said. "Who's asking?"

"I can see you're an inquisitive fellow. Perhaps I may take a minute of your time to pique your interest?" He didn't wait for a response, "Imagine after a hard day's work, reclining by the fireplace, feet up, you look to your bookshelf and there, in illustrious glory, the whole Britannica Encyclopedia Series!"

"Oh," Noah said. "No, but thanks. That indeed sounds quite nice, but honestly you came to the wrong place. We sincerely don't have a dime to spare."

Nodding in apologetic sympathy, Ed continued, "Very well, here, take a pamphlet in case your situation changes." From inside his suit pocket, he procured a pamphlet. He stepped up close to Noah and opened it towards him. He winked. At first Noah didn't look at the pamphlet but frowned at the man's behavior. But when he saw the pamphlet, he understood. Clipped inside was a handwritten note: "I appreciate an honest man looking to make an honest buck." A phone number was listed and "call Monday, ask for Valerie, tell her you are requesting details regarding 'Operation Panzerfäust.'"

"You just give that number a call if you want to make a deal," Ed said, placing his hand on Noah's arm with another wink. "You understand?"

"I do, thank you," Noah confirmed.

The man gave a courteous farewell to Eleanor and jumped in his car. They waved goodbye. Captain escorted the LeBaron back to the tree line where he resumed his lounging.

Eleanor said, "Strange. He must make a lot of money selling books to wear a suit like that with a car that matches." Noah stashed the pamphlet in the back pocket of his jeans.

"Yeah," he muttered, "suppose so."

Eleanor came to his side and put her arm around him. "One nice thing about having no money, it provides an honest refusal." She looked up at him and smiled.

"Very true," Noah affirmed.

"I'm headed over to Mother's. The boys are there now." Noah stared blankly. "It's pie baking day," she reminded him.

"You and the boys are helping Grandma now?" Noah asked.

She nodded and with a smile said, "Your mother already has the boys out back cutting the rhubarb."

"I was just going to head down to the cemetery—see if the seeds are germinating."

"Okay, dear," Eleanor gave him a kiss on the cheek. "Maybe hang up a sign at the end of the lane that says, 'No Soliciting.'"

Noah smiled. "Okay, Ella."

Once alone, Noah fetched a shovel from the shed, placed it in the truck-bed, and drove down to the prairie. He parked next to the barbed wire fence post that ran along the roadside. The country road was empty from horizon to horizon. From under his seat, he grabbed the lantern he had purchased at Traders Co. He stowed it with the shovel in the hollow of a decaying black locust, which grew behind the graves.

As he walked back to his truck, he passed the stone markers just as he had scores of other times. This time a chill ran down his spine, and the words from the service the night before came to his lips, "The earth did quake; and the rocks were rent, and the tombs..." He shuddered, shook off the chill, and drove home.

***

Rhubarb apple pie cooled on the summer kitchen's window sill. The boys, excused from their baking obligations, had taken up a game of catch in the front yard under the catalpas. Noah wandered from the shed, drawn out like a bee to a flower, by the intoxicating aroma wafting from the sill. The rhythmic sound of baseball smacking leather filled his ears. From within the summer kitchen, Eleanor saw her husband. She saw a strange expression on his face—a distraught gaze. He began to rub his chest as though a pain ailed him. She came out to him.

"Are you alright?" she asked.

"I spent the last hour walking around the barnyard imagining dollar signs on everything," Noah said exasperated. "It's the smell of the pie, the boys in the yard, even the depressing irony of Captain pining under the pines. I can't bear the thought of losing it all."

"We would still have each other," his wife offered, "and it's not the *physical* location that makes a home."

"I don't know, Ella, I don't know." He shook his head and put an arm around her waist. "I think much of this is wrapped up in who we are." He held his free arm out to capture the setting. "Sure, it doesn't define us, but you cannot deny the influence this place has on our lives."

"That's true."

"I can't lose that, Eleanor. I won't." Noah clenched his fist.

Eleanor looked uncertain. "Why don't you come inside? Spend time with me while I help your mother with Easter eggs. We finished the pies; maybe we can entice Mother to give us a slice." She took his hand and smiled.

"Alright," Noah agreed. He hollered at the boys, "Sons, want to help with the eggs?"

"Not five anymore, Dad; already told Mom that," Jonah yelled back without pausing in his sport.

Noah and Eleanor exchanged glances and the two laughed. Together they went back inside.

***

The night was lit by a full moon; silver light casted shadows in the dark. Noah kept moving about under the sheets.

"What's the matter, Noah?"

"Nothing, Ella. I'm just going to get some water. Go back to sleep."

He got out of bed and stood by the window sill. A shiver passed over him though the night was warm. In the kitchen, he took a glass of water in an attempt to calm his nerves, but a chill continued to crawl down his back. *Tick-tock-tick-tock* the clock called from the living room, and a rocking chair and lamp drew him in. From the side-table he picked up his Bible and opened to the reading from the Good Friday service. Before reading anything, he closed the Bible, holding the spot with his fingers, and turned his eyes away.

Minutes passed as he sat in the rocker, a twilight sleep flitting on his eyelids. The Bible slid lower and lower where it rested on his knee. A slip and a bump startled him back again. The Bible had toppled to the floor and was laid open to the spot he had marked. "The earth did quake; and the rocks were rent; and the tombs were opened." The words seared his sleepy eyes. Noah frowned at the passage.

"Fine, have it your way," he muttered, setting the Bible back on the side-table. He reached to switch off the lamp when the *tick* of the clock caught his ear again—the hands close to meeting at midnight. Taking it from the wall he advanced the hands past the hour of twelve o'clock to one o'clock. No longer shivering, he switched the lamp off, went back into the bedroom, closed the blinds, and went to sleep.

4

"RISE AND SHINE, up an' at em'!" Noah yelled up the stairs. The boys' clock read 5:00 a.m. Jonah glared at the door, rolled over, and wrapped his pillow over his head.

Reinhardt sat up screwing a knuckle into his eye. "Dad, it's five in the morning!"

"No, it's six!"

"Dad, look again! The clock says five!"

"Daylight savings, son. 'Spring ahead.'"

Jonah exhaled a guttural sigh, "Oh, no."

"Daylight savings?" the younger said, looking at the clock. "Why didn't anyone tell me?" He threw himself down on his pillow.

The darkness outside the windows slowly turned to grey, and the morning birds began their songs. Again, Noah hollered up the stairs, "You boys about dressed? We're leaving soon."

Reinhardt whispered to Jonah, "Is Dad losing it?"

Jonah nodded with a confused sleepy look and yelled towards their open bedroom door, "Dad, it's only five—I mean six-thirty... Whatever time it is, it's early! Where' we going so early on a Sunday?"

"Sonrise Service starts at seven!"

Reinhardt rolled out of bed and fell with a clunk on the floor, and Jonah threw off his blankets. Like tornados, both boys tore across the room to the neglected calendar on their wall. Ripping off the March page, their eyes fell to the first Sunday in the month: April 3rd 1988, and sure enough written in the box were both "Easter" and "Daylight Savings." Blinking in disbelief, they took in the shock.

"Does it happen every year like this?" Reinhardt asked.

"Never in all my life."

***

The church had a clock tower with faces on all four sides; the time read 7:05 as the family hurried in.

The church was built in the early 19th century and had been renovated more than once. The result was that of both beauty and oddities: beauty captured in the stained-glass windows, wood paneling and arched doorways, and the oddities observed in crooked corners in the basement corridors, lopsided stairwells, and a shortage of plumbing to sustain the Christmas and Easter demand.

After the service, Noah was speaking with the pastor.

"We could assist," Pastor John offered.

"No, I've decided. We're selling it," Noah said firmly. "This is the most practical way. You told me your brother still works for Wood-Mizer?"

Pastor John nodded, "Yes, and he's still hiring. Are you considering?"

Noah scratched his chin hairs as he looked down at the floor. "Yeah, I need to pursue options."

"Are you headed to Indianapolis tomorrow?"

"First thing in the morning."

"I'll phone him up and let you know," said the pastor as he jotted on a sheet of paper from a pocket-notebook. "His phone and office address." Noah accepted the paper with thanks. The pastor turned his attention to Jonah who had just snuck up quietly beside his dad. "Jonah, how are those Berkshires this year?"

"Good, Pastor John. We've had several strong litters, right Dad?"

"Yes, a good number this year," Noah said.

Jonah continued, "Before you know it, we'll be weaning the little Berks' in the field."

"Planting oats, cutting clover, full tilt ahead," Noah said.

"Full tilt ahead," Jonah confirmed.

Pastor John smiled. "I'm glad to hear. I can attest first hand to the delicious fruits of your labors."

Jonah nodded in thanks.

"You and your wife will have to come by for dinner sometime," Noah said.

"Most definitely; will we see you at the festival today?"

"Yes, we'll be by this afternoon. My mother is providing pies for the pie-wheel raffle."

"Excellent, let's be sure to chat more then. I'll call my brother after second service. But excuse me, I want to catch some others before they leave."

"Sounds good, and thanks again," Noah waved the note.

"Grateful to help, Noah, see you this afternoon." Pastor John said and soon was engaged with other congregants.

"What's that?" asked Jonah, pointing to the scrap of paper in Noah's hand.

"An address," Noah said, staring in thought. "Pastor John has a brother in Indiana." Pocketing the note, he looked to his son. "Where's your mom?"

"She asked me to get you; they're waiting in the truck."

***

Arriving back home, Noah asked, "Will you boys please take care of the Berks'?"

"Sure, Dad."

Their mom yelled from the kitchen, "Change out of your church clothes first, boys!"

The boys hurried upstairs to change. Eleanor came out to the porch where Noah was fidgeting with the swing. "You had something on your mind on the drive home; what did you talk to Pastor John about?"

"I told him our situation. Of course he wants to help, but I insisted it's time I make a move. Told him I was headed to Indiana to sell the Wood-Mizer. Do you remember his brother? He's still hiring; maybe able to set me up with a job."

"Would that mean moving to Indiana?"

"It would be nearly three hours commute one way," Noah frowned.

"When will you break it to the boys?"

"Only if it becomes a reality."

"They aren't… Jonah isn't going to handle that well."

"I know."

Eleanor came to his side. Together they looked out over the lawn.

"We'll figure it out, dear, one day at a time." She gave her husband a kiss; that same moment, the boys came out.

"Hey you two, get a room." Jonah said as he and Reinhardt headed to the barn.

"I have to help your mother pack up the pies." Eleanor said, with a final affectionate squeeze.

Noah stood alone on the porch for a minute. "Cap'n, you under there?" He stomped on the porch boards. There was no sound.

From his wallet, he fetched the slip of paper Ed had given him the day before. At the hallway phone he dialed the number. It went to the "Heinrich's Ratskeller" answering machine. Noah hung up. "Heinrich's?" he questioned out loud. He opened the telephone book and thumbed through the Yellow Pages, saw that the number from Ed matched the restaurant's, and called a second time. Again, after ringing, it went to "Heinrich's" answering machine. He left a message on the recording: "Hey, this is Mr. Brandtmeyer calling for Al. Uh, I got his message yesterday and regret to inform him I was not able to um… I do not have anything for selling. I thought I did, but I don't. I will not be able to move forward with any job offers at this time. Really appreciate your time. If this is the wrong number, my apologies. Good-day." He hung up.

"Who was that?"

Noah jumped. Reinhardt was standing in the doorway. "Heinrich's," Noah said and stuffed the paper slip into his pocket. "You're already finished with the feeding?"

"I wanted my pocket knife. I forgot it." He fetched it from the mudroom adjacent to the front door. "Dad, will there be brats and sauerkraut at the festival?"

"Huh?"

"You ordered from Heinrich's?"

"Oh, no. No, we'll eat at the festival. Run along now. I'll be out in just a minute." Noah watched his son head back outside, then exhaled realizing he had been holding his breath. "Lord, help me."

***

When they had finished tending the farm, they all loaded into the Chevy. The boys rode in the truck-bed to keep the pie boxes stable. Their parents and Grandma rode in the cab. They headed back into town for the annual Springfest held at the local park. A big tent with blue and white stripes was pitched on the grass. Part of the parking lot was petitioned off with tasseled rope where a large red dunk tank was set up; some poor soul in a full body wetsuit was clambering back upon the seat.

After the Brandtmeyers finished eating under the big tent, Jonah said, "I'm going to get a closer look at this dunk tank."

"Can I come along?" Reinhardt asked.

"Come on." Jonah waved as he started off.

Near the dunk tank several treat stations had been set up as well. Reinhardt stood by a candy stand looking at the menu. A whirling cotton candy machine caught his gaze.

Jonah watched as a girl about his age attempted to hit the dunk tank target. She threw three balls, missing every time. Without hesitation she purchased three more and blew through them as quickly as her first set, still missing the mark.

"Nice try," Jonah said to her.

"It's not easy," she said.

"Sure it is."

"Let's see you do it."

"Naw, I'm not going to waste my money to throw a ball," Jonah defended.

"Oh, sure, I see. Put your money where your mouth is."

"Really, I can throw balls at targets all day long for free."

"Yeah, but dunking the person is the point. I want to see you do it; I'll buy you the balls."

"No, that's okay."

She was already handing money to the attendee and collected the balls.

"Well thanks," Jonah said, "I'll do it in one." He took one of the baseballs and tossed it lightly up in his hand. The dunk tank apparatus consisted of a large red tank about five feet high with a net around the top, which protected the individual within from a terrible shot. Jonah took his stance, made eye contact with the dunkee, gave a nod, the wind up and *smack*! A solid blow to the target dropped the dunkee into the water.

"Hot damn! Well done," The girl applauded, dropping the extra balls. Jonah smiled and picked them up.

"Did you want to try again?" he asked.

"No thanks."

"Is it alright if I give them to my little brother then?"

"Absolutely."

"Here Reinhardt, have a try." Jonah called over to Reinhardt where he still stood salivating for cotton candy. He jogged over and took the balls as if they had been unearthed treasure.

"How did you buy these?"

"Shut up, Reiner; just go throw it at the target."

"What's your brother's name?"

"Reinhardt," Reinhardt blurted out before Jonah could respond.

"But sometimes I just call him 'Reiner.' Right, Reiner?" Jonah said, and Reinhardt frowned a little. "But he doesn't like it," Jonah explained.

"I think it's a cute name—Reiner," the girl tried it out.

"That's the problem! And it sounds like 'Whiner,'" Reinhardt objected.

Jonah smiled at the comment. "Well maybe you are, now go throw the balls already." He turned his attention back to the girl. "I'm Jonah Brandtmeyer."

"Leslie Schreiber. It's nice to meet you, honestly, not just the way when people say it."

"Oh, yeah?"

49

"See, my family just moved here, and it's so nice to meet new people. What school do you go to?"

Jonah's face cringed slightly in thought. "It's like a part-time school."

"How's that work?"

"I don't meet with my class every day, Monday through Friday."

"What town is that school in?" Leslie asked.

"Oh, the town over there," Jonah waved in no particular direction, "but really it's not so much that, it's more at home."

"You're homeschooled?"

"If that's what you want to call it."

The girl was leaning slightly back with widened eyes, "I've never met a homeschooler before, you seem normal to me," she put her hand over her mouth, "I mean, it's just people say things, I don't know really."

"Oh yeah, what do they say?"

She lightly tapped on her temple. "I wouldn't have expected to talk with you, that's all. It sounds interesting. Do you have a desk at home?"

"Yes."

"And do you have to sit alone by yourself and work?"

"Sometimes."

"But that sounds so lonely."

"I'm not sitting there for hours alone; it's not like public school. Sometimes I'll spend just an hour for the whole day or, honestly, not at all." At this her eyes widened again. "And," Jonah continued, "I'm in F.F.A. That's in New Bremen, and I do more learning outdoors."

"Oh, field trips," she interjected.

"Yes, that too. We've been to the Zanesville caverns, visited the Amish at Holmes County, last year we went to the Armstrong Air and Space Museum."

"My old school went to the Dayton Art Museum last year," Leslie said.

"That's cool."

"But you don't live under a rock at all; you've been more places than me!" Leslie exclaimed, and her face looked impressed. "Let's walk around a bit," she continued, "and check things out around the festival."

"That sounds good. Hey, Reinhardt, did you hit the target?"

"No."

"Well hey, not everyone can do it. Why don't you head back to the big tent where Mom and Dad are? We'll catch up in a bit. Leslie and I are going to walk around."

***

The parents were under the big tent talking with the pastor and his wife.

"There's an old graveyard near our place, most are over one hundred years old. There's not much left of the bodies, I suppose. When it says the graves were opened and they walked around... I mean what in the world would that have looked like?" Noah asked.

"It's unclear, perhaps like Lazarus," Pastor John said, "We know through implication that he didn't 'have an odor' yet he was wrapped up in burial linens."

"Come along Eleanor, let's walk around a bit," Pastor John's wife said. The two women departed.

Pastor John smiled in farewell, and then continued speaking with Noah, "How are you two doing with all this?"

"Well, praise the Lord—Eleanor, she's very supportive. Always has been."

"'A worthy woman who can find? For her price is far above rubies.' Mr. Noah Brandtmeyer, he can." He smiled warmly.

Noah smiled at the compliment. For a few moments the two sat quietly. They watched as the lunch crowd migrated to the other end of the tent towards the pie wheel raffle. Kids and adults began placing quarters on numbers like in a game of roulette. The smallest children, oblivious to the meaning of numbers and wagers, searched the grass under the tables for fallen change.

John broke their silence, "So that new bank really means business?"

"Their management isn't playing softball. Diamond Saving and Loan knew my father and had an understanding relationship with us after his disappearance."

"What good is a life insurance policy for a man that is neither dead nor alive? There must be stipulations for this sort of thing?"

"After seven years, I can apply for a Death Claim,—"

A sudden burst of applause and clapping erupted from the other end of the tent. The first victor held up an apple lattice pie. The sound of more and more nickels, dimes, and quarters could be heard clattering on the tables as the ante upped.

"—and it's a credit life insurance policy," Noah said.

"Forgive me, I forgot the difference."

"It's insurance for the farm. The insurance is designed to pay off whatever the remainder of the farm loan is at the time of the policy holder's death."

"So, a family won't see a dime of the policy unless death is confirmed?"

"Correct, or wait seven years from the time of his assumed death."

"Your dad's disappearance... has it been two years already?"

Noah nodded. "This May."

"I miss your father; he was a jovial man—and always telling good stories."

Again they sat quietly. Reinhardt returned.

"Where's your brother?" Noah asked.

Reinhardt shrugged, "I don't know."

"Hmm, that reminds me, I spoke with my brother in Indiana," John added. "They're open to an interview."

"Good," Noah said. "Hey Reinhardt, your grandmother is over by the pie wheel—raffle's started, why don't you see if she needs any help?" Noah watched Reinhardt until he was out of earshot. "I haven't broken the news to my sons."

"Oh, sorry," Pastor John said, "I hope I didn't..."

"No, not at all," Noah waved his hand as if to brush the matter aside, "Reinhardt, he's—well, he's a bit aloof anyways."

"I don't want to encourage you to take the job."

Noah cocked his head. "How do you mean?"

"Selfish reasons—I don't actually want you to move away. Your community is here."

"Thanks, John. If we leave, it will have been entirely your fault," Noah jested.

***

From a distance Leslie and Jonah watched the pie wheel raffle taking place under the big tent. They had meandered around, Leslie bought cotton candy, Jonah indulged in most of it, and Reinhardt was not around to get any. Together the two sat on a park bench, they were within view of the large spinning wheel that *ti-ti-ti-ti-ti-ti-ti-ticked* as it spun round and round until it stopped on a number. Cheering went up as some lucky gambler won a pie—the proceeds were donated to a local charity.

"Do you prefer pie or cake?" Leslie asked.

"Hmm, pie. What about you?"

"Cake. For my birthday I asked for a three-tiered cake! Two tiers for candles and car keys on top."

"You got a car for your birthday?" Jonah looked incredulous.

"Hasn't happened yet..." Leslie trailed off into a big smile.

"How old are you?"

"I'm sixteen!"

"You have your driver's license?"

"I'm sixteen tomorrow! And I *will* have my driver's license. My mom's taking me out of school tomorrow to get it." She wore a huge smile. The cotton candy stained her lips and teeth a light blue.

"Oh yeah? I'll believe it when I see it," Jonah smirked.

"What, you don't think I can parallel park? It's so easy." She rolled her eyes.

"I just said I'll believe it when I see it. I don't know a thing about your driving. I know it's easy, I drive tractors and trucks all the time."

"So you're already sixteen?"

"Oh, uh almost, I drive our farm truck and tractors some, but—you know," he shrugged coolly, "not quite street legal."

Again Leslie had an impressed look. "But, cars do go a lot faster." She got an idea, "I'll prove it to you."

"That cars go a lot faster?"

"Well, both!" She giggled, "I meant I'll prove to you I'll get my license. I'll come by. Where do you live?"

"West, take Moulton Angle, left at Moulton New Knoxville, and we're on the right just before Wiefenbach Road."

"I may be able to drive, but I may need those directions again. I mean, when we lived in Cincinnati I was learning the roads, but here everything is so little—the streets. It's almost harder to know where you are."

"I can write it down. Do you have any paper?"

She opened her sequin studded purse and pulled out an old J.C. Penny's receipt and a purple gel pen. "Write it on the back of this."

He did so as she continued talking, explaining that the receipt was for her new bedazzled purse: an early birthday present ready to house a beautiful new glossy driver's license.

"Here you go." He handed her his address.

"Thanks, Jonah!"

Pedestrian traffic started to increase around their bench as the crowd around the pie wheel began to disperse. "Hey, it looks like they raffled all the pies. I better find my grandma."

"Alright, I better get going myself," Leslie said. "It was so nice meeting you." She smiled again—a bit of blue lingered about her lips.

Jonah rubbed the tip of his right ear; it was burning hot. "Likewise. And happy birthday if I don't see you again."

"Oh, you'll see me again." She waved the scrawled receipt in the air and then skipped off.

Jonah rubbed his chin and mouth to conceal a smile. "Hot damn," he mused and wandered back to the big tent to find his family.

***

That evening in the living room Jonah said to his dad, "I met a girl at the festival today; she's turning sixteen. She's getting a car for her birthday. Isn't that wild?"

"Who's the girl?"

"Leslie Schreiber."

"Schreiber?" he questioned. "Eleanor!" he called into the other room, "Where have I heard the name 'Schreiber?'"

"Mr. Don Schreiber?" Eleanor asked.

Some of the color left Noah's cheeks. "Oh, right," he mumbled. "Well, there are lots of Schreiber's no doubt."

"She said they've only recently moved here," Jonah said. "Do you know her parents?"

"I'm not sure," Noah paused for a moment. "Maybe I can find out tomorrow. What's she like?"

"She was cool. I invited her to drive by when she gets her license. Can't throw worth a damn."

Noah let out a chuckle and shook his head. "Watch your language son, but I believe you. Men love throwing things, so much so we've made 'playing catch' a game. Take a woman for contrast though; she won't even toss you the T.V. remote from across the couch."

"I heard that!" Eleanor called in protest from the other room.

5

"ONE-TENTH," Noah said, dumping the rain gauge. "Rain Friday," he eyed Jonah, "rain Friday night," he clarified. "Rain Sunday night." He nodded with approval. "Come along, Jonah."

The two got into the truck and drove down the lane to the woods. An earthy smell of dirt and fungus rose from the ground. Worms slimed the lane taking refuge from the recent rainfall. Their shapes were like the scattering of little bits of intestines. And the potholes next to these were miniature mortar blasts—Noah swerved to miss a large one.

"Dad, this lane could use grading."

"Good observation, son. It really needs fresh gravel and gravel costs money."

They pulled up to the Quonset. "Hop out and open the bay doors, please," Noah instructed. With doors open, Noah backed the truck up to the LT-40 Wood-Mizer. "Does the hitch need raised?" Noah called out the truck window.

"We're hooking her up?" Jonah questioned.

"Trying to, does the hitch need raised?"

"Yes."

"Jack her on up."

When the sawmill had been hitched and secured, Jonah exclaimed, "We're... we're firing her up, Dad!?"

"Well, not exactly," Noah bent down to take a pressure reading on the Wood-Mizer's tires. Satisfied with the pressure, he turned his attention back towards his son, "Taking it to Indiana."

"Big job in Indiana? You're going to do it?"

Noah swallowed hard, "There's a job of sorts... but, no son, I'm selling the sawmill back to Wood-Mizer."

"What!?" Jonah's whole countenance went up in a flame of rage.

"I'm sorry, son. It's an expense we can't keep any longer."

"It's Granddad's! You're giving up on him? I didn't even get to mill any wood!"

"It isn't like that at all. I thought you knew!"

"If you said we were selling her, I didn't hear."

"I'm sorry. We've had it nearly untouched for two years. That's two years we've been making payments on it. If it ever was a cash cow, it's a cash hog now."

Jonah clambered into the LT-40's seat and touched all the levers of the control box. "It's still a piece of Granddad and you're going to let that go." He came down from the operators chair and kicked the tires. "What else of Granddad's are you going to get rid of?"

"Drop it, son."

"What, are you gonna' get rid of Captain next?" His voice was rising.

"Jonah, you're out of line—"

"Burn down his shop office?"

"You better watch that mouth, or I'll straighten you out." Noah put his hand on his belt.

Jonah clenched his jaw shut. For a moment, father and son were locked in a stand-off. Jonah backed down and muttered in a low voice, "Do you need me for anything else?"

"No, just check on the Berkshires later."

Jonah walked to the back of the Quonset and closed himself in Granddad's old shop office.

Noah sighed and returned to the farmyard where he picked up Eleanor. She was standing on the porch. Noah came around and opened the cab door of the truck for her.

"All set," he called up to her where she stood.

Walking down the porch steps, she asked, "Where's Jonah?"

Noah waved to the east. "He's there."

"What's wrong?"

"He's pretty upset to see the Wood-Mizer go."

"Did you explain why?"

"Tried to."

His arms rested on the open sill of the cab door with shoulders sagging and head swaying. "I'll have to sit him down this evening and really explain our situation."

"I think that would be wise." She smiled and put her hand on his shoulder. "One thing at a time."

Reinhardt walked up with eggs in a bushel basket.

"What are you explaining this evening?" he asked. "And where are you going with Granddad's Wood-Mizer?"

Noah looked to Eleanor. Eleanor whispered, "Don't look at me."

"I'll sit you both down this evening. We'll discuss a few farm matters. But suffice it to say, the Wood-Mizer is being sold. Now before you get upset, realize it is what your granddad would have wanted under the circumstances."

Reinhardt nodded, and asked, "Will we get another one someday? For Jonah's sake?"

Noah put his hand on Reinhardt's shoulder and looked him in the eyes. "That's something to pray for." Then he looked at the basket his son was holding. "Good egg collection this morning?"

"Yeah, fifteen, I think," Reinhardt said looking into his basket.

"Why don't you take those over to the summer kitchen for your grandmother," Noah said.

"And Reinhardt," Eleanor added, "spend some time with her, will you please? We'll be gone several hours."

"Okay, sure thing. Where's Jonah?"

"At the woods," Noah said.

Eleanor gave her son a hug then got into the truck cab. "Take care, Reinhardt! Love you."

Noah also got in and started the engine. "Love you, son. We should be back late this afternoon."

"Okay Dad, bye. Bye, Mom." He waved farewell as they drove the Chevy with the sawmill down the lane.

Reinhardt stood in the farmyard taking in the dewy air. The grass was green again and soon would need to be mowed but not today. He went to the summer kitchen and knocked at the door.

"Grandma!"

"Come on in."

Reinhardt entered the sunny summer kitchen.

"I brought you some eggs." He set the basket down and pulled off his boots.

"Thanks, my dear."

"What are you doing today?"

"Did you have breakfast already?"

"Yes."

"I'll make some lunch later; in the meantime, I was just preparing to work in the garden."

She took up the basket of eggs and worked briefly in the kitchen. The summer kitchen had been renovated to accommodate living quarters. On the right side was a small sitting area and dominating the main space an old quilting rack was set with a quilt mid-stitch. Reinhardt looked over the in-progress cross-stitching. Against the wall of the sitting area a large glass paned hutch displayed stacks of colorful quilts of every pattern: Jacob's ladder, basket, double T, Carolina lily, double wedding ring, and log cabin. "How many quilts did you make last year, Grandma?"

"Sixteen."

"Is that a record?"

"Indeed, it is. I'll probably make sixteen or more this year, Lord willing. It keeps my mind occupied and the hands busy. Alright, come along now." She put on a sun hat and Reinhardt pulled his boots back on. Together they went around to the garden shed on the west side of the summer kitchen. They fetched hoe and trowel and began the assault on weeds that had ravaged what remained from last fall.

"It'll be a fine season for gardening and a warm spring; though, there will be another frost or two as of yet."

"How can you know that?" asked Reinhardt.

"You don't get arthritis without some benefits—barometer, weather forecaster," she winked, "and then there's the Farmers' Almanac."

Reinhardt's eyebrows rose in wonder. "And will we have some big old heirlooms and snap peas?"

"Indeed, we shall. You'll have to be on hornworm duty though."

"Are those the huge green ones with the spike on their butt and poop the shape of miniature grenades?"

Grandma chuckled, "Yes, those are the ones."

"I do love smashing a plump hornworm." Reinhardt smiled.

The morning waned and the sun rose high overhead.

"Where's your brother?" Grandma asked. She took off her gardening gloves and dabbed her forehead with a lace handkerchief.

"I don't know. I think Mom and Dad said something about him being at the woods."

"It's about lunchtime. I'll fix you and Jonah sandwiches."

Indoors, Grandma stacked two dogwoods: with Brandtmeyer's acorn-finished pork, cucumbers pickled in the cellar, a local cheese from a neighboring farm, all hugged between two fresh baked slices of French bread lathered in homemade mayonnaise, mustard, and butter. These with the remains of Easter's hardboiled eggs and two glass bottles of Frostop root beer—"These root beers were your granddad's favorites"—and a canteen of water she placed in a wicker basket and gave to Reinhardt. "There you are, all your granddad's favorites, but your granddad's favorite treat this time of year was a good spring morel. When you have finished eating, go find some in the woods; put them in this basket and bring 'em back. I'll fry them up for dinner tonight."

"You got it Grandma, thanks, love you. See you later," Reinhardt called as he trotted out the front door and across the farmyard. The orchard along the lane was vibrant with pink blossoms like great explosions of fireworks frozen in time. From a distance, the woods had begun to look thicker with new growth, but as he drew nearer the individual trees were only budding. Against the edge of the woods, the corrugated surface of the arched Quonset glinted brilliantly in the afternoon sun.

Reinhardt found Jonah sitting at Granddad's old desk.

"Sandwiches, courtesy of Grandma." Reinhardt set the load down on the desk.

Jonah opened the basket lid and inhaled the delicious scent. "What a good grandma!" He un-wrapped a sandwich and began to devour it. Reinhardt did likewise. For a few minutes they sat eating their sandwiches: Jonah at the desk and Reinhardt, with his feet up on a box, sat at the couch.

Reinhardt looked around the old office space. A spade, a post-hole shovel, a broken peavey, and the likes slumped against one corner next to the book shelf. On the opposite side the trash bin was overflowing like a spring fountain. Newspaper scraps, seed bags, feed bags, and grime carpeted the concrete floor. A small leak in the roof watered a spot on the floor and an oat seed had sprouted up from a damp patch of black rot. Cobwebs hung in every corner. Bottles lined every ledge. A stack of chicken crates prevented the door to the bay area from opening all the way. On the walls hung a few old framed photos—one of Granddad himself looking dapper and confident as he posed with his pristine LT-40 Wood-Mizer. The glass in the frame was broken; shards laid on the floor below. There also hung on the wall a faded calendar from '86 with the April month exposed.

"For as much time as you spend out here, you should tidy up the place," Reinhardt said.

"I have in the past, but it just gets messy again. Every season this office turns more and more into a storage shed."

"Toss me one of the eggs, please." Reinhardt peeled his egg, putting the shells on his sandwich wrapper. "Hey Jonah, Grandma wants us to search for morels after this."

"Does she think they'll already be out?"

"Yeah, she was talking about it being a mild spring for it— said how they were Granddad's favorite treat this time of year."

"I know." Jonah took the last dated journal down from a long row on the shelf. "Listen to what he wrote in his last journal, '85's, he records where he found the sneaky mushrooms." He flipped through some pages. "Here's one, this isn't the one I wanted to show you but it's funny, this one is from late May: 'Everyone knows April showers bring May flowers but that's when the morel hunter heads north of the sinkhole, for that's the morel hot spot! Fry them up at home and drink them with a Frostop!'"

"That sounds disgusting." Reinhardt's face contorted into mock vomiting.

"Who knows, maybe when you get older your taste buds go crazy?" Jonah was flipping through the pages again. "But here's the one for us now: 'When an early spring prevails, morel mushrooms unveil, search the southern slopes to where the morels elope.' I think he had found morels on the south edge; more than once, I know I was with him at least one time," Jonah said, closing the journal.

"I liked Granddad's rhyme."

"Yeah, he was always like that, just a happy Granddad."

"What's elope mean?"

"I think he means, 'where they run off,' or like, 'where they're hiding.'"

Reinhardt searched the wicker basket. "Well then the bottle opener has 'eloped' too. I don't see one in the basket." He set the two Frostops on the desk.

"That's because Grandma knows Granddad has one or two in here." Jonah pulled open the desk drawer and rummaged around. "I don't see one in here. Is it in-between those couch cushions?"

Reinhardt pulled the cushions off the couch and a mouse came running out. They watched it scurry until it became lost in the debris.

"Jonah, this place has really gone to seed."

"Tell me about it. Any luck in the couch?"

"No, it's not here."

"That's lame, well come on. Let's leave the root beer on the shelf and maybe we'll find an opener later." He placed the two bottles on the shelf along with Journal '85. The shelf of journals was the only space in the whole office that was kempt.

"Let's get those mushrooms," Jonah said.

"Do you know where he means?"

"I know he means the southern border of the woods from the rhyme."

"Okay, but anything more specific?"

"We also know they grow around decaying trees. We have a lot to go on."

Branches were shooting supple new leaves by the thousands. These tiny leaves allowed sunlight to pour through to the woodland floor causing a luscious undergrowth to thrive. Dense patches of white clover rolled gently across the landscape mixed with multiple delicate purple flowers: clusters of the five petal Blue Phlox, Violets shaped like small butterflies, and, "Are these nettles?"

"Purple Dead Nettle? Maybe." Jonah took a closer look at the proud little flower. "It's Henbit."

"So many purple flowers!" Reinhardt exclaimed. "But not a morel in sight. Here's another one, what are these?" Reinhardt crouched down gently lifting the blooms that were otherwise angled down towards the earth.

"Jacob's Ladder."

"Jacob's Ladder? That's one of Grandma's quilt designs. Do you think it gets its name from these?"

"I have no idea. Ask Grandma."

Reinhardt picked a couple and put them in his front pocket. At the southern edge of the woods, the two crept among the tall golden Ragwort and, "What are these white ones?"

"Oxeye Daisies, they're out early this year; that's good news for us."

"How do you know the names of everything," Reinhardt asked.

"Granddad—we spent a lot of time in the woods. He was right here you know—at least three years ago... three years ago to this very season, looking for morels; probably wearing his wrist watch." He dug under the tall Ragwort, flowers, and undergrowth.

"Jonah, you won't find them *under* the leaves."

"I know. I was looking for something else," Jonah said vaguely while wiping his nose on his sleeve.

They spent an hour in quiet hunting. All was warm, pleasant and breezy—the quintessential Ohio spring day. At one point some loud buzzing bees threatened to sting Jonah, and at another point Reinhardt stumbled through a spot of tall Ragwort and yelled, "Jonah! A spider bit me. I think it was poisonous!"

"Where's the spider; what did he look like?" Jonah asked.

"I don't know where the little sucker went, but he was big, black, and bright yellow."

His older brother looked at the tattered remains of the web dangling in the weed. "You're fine, Reinhardt, look," Jonah pointed to a spot on the web. "See that zig-zaggy design right there?" A prominent zig-zag pattern on the center part of what was left of the web was clearly visible. "That's a Gardener Spider's trademark or I'm not my granddad's namesake. You're fine."

Reinhardt took comfort in the way Jonah spoke with such informed authority on the matter. "I suppose it is a small bite after all," he said while looking at a red dot on his arm and added, "come to think of it, that may just be a prick from a thorn."

"Ha," Jonah laughed. "Oh, Reinhardt, sometimes I wonder about you."

They continued their hunt for the mushrooms again in quiet earnest. After another hour, Reinhardt broke the silent searching. "Some grandparents!"

"What do you mean?"

"First Grandma tells me they're ready, and then Granddad says where. What do we find? Nothing."

"Morels are like that, near impossible to find," Jonah said.

"Morels and Granddad alike, huh?"

"That's the most intelligent thing I've ever heard you say."

6

As THE BOYS came up from the woods, they saw a car turn off the road into their lane. It cut the corner early and left a rut in the green grass. Captain came out from his hiding and was watching the car with a cocked head.

"That's not our parents," Reinhardt said.

"Obviously not," Jonah confirmed. "This fellow can't drive worth a damn; did you see how he nearly went into the ditch? Even Captain doesn't know what to make of it. Come on, I'll race you there, and we can run this jokester off before he bothers Grandma."

Together they took off. Reinhardt kept up with Jonah until the fencepost corner where Jonah sprinted ahead. The person in the car became visible.

"Leslie!" Jonah hollered. "So, look at you, driving. I see and believe."

She got out of the snazzy '87 Buick Regal, face beaming. "Pretty slick, I know." She opened her sequined purse and caught the afternoon sun off the surface of her freshly laminated driver's license.

"Incredible," Jonah nodded.

Reinhardt came up behind them out of breath. "Thirsty. Jonah, we forgot our root beers."

"Oh yeah, Reinhardt, you met Leslie—Leslie, Reinhardt. Reinhardt, Leslie. We forgot our Frostops back over there," Jonah waved randomly, "but that's okay."

"I could drive you there, or better yet, we could go into town! A root beer float sounds good," Leslie said.

Jonah glanced around then said, "I like it. Reinhardt, go get my wallet from my night stand. We'll go, but I need to check on our Berkshires first."

"What's Berkshires?"

"Just our pigs, Berkshire is the breed. We've got some piglets. Do you like little baby pigs?"

"I love anything that's a baby!"

"Great." Jonah smiled.

She wrinkled her nose. "But are they stinky?"

"You'll have to tell me. Come on."

In the farrowing barn the piglets were a lively bunch. Some chased each other about interrupting the ones snoozing in the straw. One piglet ran across two little piglets that were burrowed down deep in the straw; all three for a moment were a jumbled mess of hooves and squeals. Once the instigator got right-side-up again he was quick to be off running around, while the others nestled back down. Their pink noses rested so close to one another's that they touched.

"Aww look, it's like they're kissing." The girl pointed to the pair.

"Yeah, they're a snuggly bunch. Is it too stinky for you?"

"It's a little stinky," she admitted.

"Do you want to come up in the loft?" Jonah stood at the base of the ladder. "Won't be as smelly up there."

The girl looked up the ladder towards the loft. "It looks dark up there."

"Once I open a hatch, it's not too bad."

"I'll watch the pigs from here."

"Okay, well I'm going to throw corncobs out the back. Once the sows go out, we can catch a piglet for you to pet if you want."

"Really? That would be great."

While Jonah was in the loft, Reinhardt returned. He looked at the girl. "Is Jonah up top?"

"Yeah."

He looked into the stalls. "Bedding looks fresh enough, you think?"

"I wouldn't know. What's bedding? The hay?"

"Well, it's straw, but yeah, I just mean the pens look clean. Excuse me; I have to check their water." Reinhardt went back out around the side of the barn.

"Jonah," she called up the hatch, "the big momma pigs are going out the back. Are you coming back down?"

Suddenly his head poked over the loft's edge. "Just now, one moment," he said. Soon he was descending the ladder. The girl observed his deft movements.

"The guys in my gym class, some of them are so awkward," Leslie said.

"Huh?"

She smiled. "When you move around and work, it's obvious you know what you're doing."

"Oh, thanks." He fumbled with the latch to the stall; the tips of his ears started to burn. "Tell me that right before I try catching a piglet." He got the latch open with a sudden violent shake—"Heh, finicky old latch"—and went for one of the nesting piglets, but they lunged away from him and he missed.

She laughed. "I guess your agility training comes from real world experiences, not dodging balls in a gymnasium."

"Where's that little rascal that was running around earlier?" He brushed his hands around in the straw. "See, he'll be all tuckered out now. Ah-ha!" Jonah took a quick step and grabbed, and up from the straw hoisted his prize, "Gotcha'." The black and white Berkshire let out a squeal of protest, but in Jonah's practiced arms he calmed down.

"Look at his little nose; he's so adorable," Leslie said as she tried to pet it.

"Here, try this." Jonah pushed down on the piglet's snout and it fought back. Leslie did likewise. With the same determination the piglet rooted up. The more she pushed down the more it pushed back.

"That's so cute! Why does he do that?"

"It's rooting—just an instinct like human babies grabbing things with their hands."

She continued fondling over the piglet, petting the coarse black coat or trying to scratch the white patch on its face.

"Do you want to try holding him?"

"Oh no, too scared I'd drop him."

At that moment Reinhardt returned. "I think the pens look clean enough."

"Yeah," Jonah agreed. He set the piglet down in the straw.

"I topped off the water."

"So, we're all set?" Leslie asked.

Jonah was pulling the stall door against the latch. "Yeah, we're all set. Reinhardt, grab me a piece of twine, this latch is getting finicky." A barrel sat in the aisle that held discarded twine from the straw bales used for bedding, and from this Reinhardt grabbed a piece. Jonah fashioned a square knot to hold the gate closed. "And did you grab my wallet?"

"Yeah." Reinhardt handed Jonah his wallet.

He peeked within the billfold and cringed. "Ha, Reinhardt grabbed my wrong wallet."

"You have two wall—?"

"Shut up, Reiner. Hey look, why don't you two hop in the car? I'll be right back; I call shotgun."

Jonah darted into the house. In his parents' room he pinched a five-dollar bill from a small stack of small bills hidden in the back of his dad's underwear drawer.

Back outside, Leslie was waiting in the driver's seat, and Reinhardt had the back seat door open but was waiting outside the car.

"Alright, that should do it," Jonah said, as he came to the car, holding up his wallet. "Let's go."

He was about to enter "shot-gun" when Reinhardt asked, "Should I tell Grandma we're leaving?"

"You didn't already?" Reinhardt shook his head. Jonah already had one leg in the car door. "I thought you were showing her the Jacob's Ladder flowers?"

"Oh! I forgot all about them." Reinhardt dug the flowers out of this shirt pocket. They were sad, wilted, and brown.

Jonah laughed. "Come on, let's go already." With that he hopped in and closed the door.

Reinhardt hesitated, looking at the sad bouquet, but when Leslie turned on the engine, he mumbled something about "Don't leave yet," dropped the vegetation, and jumped in.

"Buckle up everyone." The car creeped down the lane and gravel crunched under the wheels. They rolled the windows down—fresh air flooded the interior.

Reinhardt waved a good-bye to Captain who had resumed his lounging. "Next time you see us we'll have some ice cream!" Reinhardt yelled out the window to him.

"Who's that?" Leslie asked.

"Our dog, Captain," said Reinhardt.

Jonah rolled his eyes. "But he's not a very good dog anymore."

"Why do you say that?" Leslie asked.

"He's an Australian shepherd. They're supposed to be good trackers, but he's never found a thing. I think he must feel like a failure," Jonah concluded.

Leslie's car reached the end of the lane. "Well, I hope you won't fail me."

"Huh?" Jonah's face reddened.

"I have no idea which way to root beer floats."

"Oh," Jonah exhaled, "right. Take a right." He turned the radio up. "This is interesting."

"This is M. C. Lyte, do you know her?" she sang along with a line of chorus, "it's so good, all about being real. Know what I mean?"

"Yeah, totally."

Leslie turned the music back down. "I actually asked for some music for my birthday, but my mom said it had a 'parental advisory.'" She rolled her eyes. "Parents, always cramping your style, or dragging you places you don't want to go."

"Ha! That's been this past year for me," Jonah said.

"Really? I'm telling you, it's constant."

"Yeah, I guess come to think of it, you're right." Jonah thought about it. "Yesterday, I'm trying to sleep, and Dad wakes us up at what was practically five a.m., for what? Church service."

"That's just like my mom, constantly trying to drag me to Mass." Leslie pulled up to a stop sign and asked, "Which way from here?"

"Turn west," Jonah looked at her expression and clarified, "turn left, then in another two or three miles we'll be in St. Marys, the ice cream parlor is at the first traffic light."

Reinhardt asked, "So you're Catholic?"

"Huh?" Leslie asked as she made a wide left turn running the passenger's side wheel off the asphalt a bit.

"Mass."

"Oh, I don't know, I mean my mom goes to Mass," Leslie explained, "but my dad goes to synagogue or at least he did in Cincinnati. He wanted to go all the way down there for Passover—couldn't get off work, which apparently has him depressed as hell, new transfer and all. But me," Leslie said resolutely, "I'm just sincere. You know what I mean? All this religious stuff just causes problems."

"Sincerity's good," Jonah agreed.

Reinhardt said with a puzzled look, "So does that mean you're Catholic or Jewish?"

Jonah turned the radio back up, drowning Reinhardt's question out; then he spoke loudly over the radio, "So, I forgot, I know you said your dad was transferred and all, but what does he do?"

7

"So, you did have the money." Mr. Don Schreiber stood by his desk holding the check up as if to inspect whether it was a forgery or not. "This definitely relieves the pressure, but don't think you're off the hook, Mr. Brandtmeyer. Am I to anticipate a timely payment next month?"

"Settle your horses, Mr. Schreiber. I made good on my word and it's only Monday." Noah turned to go. "Oh, Mr. Schreiber, my son met a girl yesterday: Leslie Schreiber. Do you know her?"

"She's my daughter."

"Hmm, well, welcome to Small Town America." Noah turned to walk out, noticing the grimace left on Mr. Schreiber's face.

Noah returned to the truck where Eleanor had remained waiting for him.

She asked, "How was our dear banker today? Was he satisfied?"

"Mr. Schreiber is a horse's—" Noah clenched his jaw, "I don't mean that." Shaking off his irritation, he continued, "I can't wait to meet his daughter."

Eleanor laughed. "Oh, goodness! One in the same? What did he say?"

Noah smiled. "I guess we gave him a good and proper welcome to our world. But I'm not concerned about it—that is, the kids causing trouble anyways."

"So now what?"

"We get ice cream."

"I meant with the loan?"

"One day at a time, Ella. Let's celebrate today's little victory with some ice cream."

"Okay, I could go for some," Eleanor said.

They pulled into the drive-thru queue. The ice cream parlor shared the last intersection in town with Certified Gas and Market. Here was the final outpost before multiple country roads winded their way into the rural landscape.

"Copacetic."

"What's that?" Eleanor asked. She was eyeing a girl walking out of the parlor holding a tray with three beverages. The girl was looking around with a lost expression.

"Did Reinhardt ask you what the word 'copacetic' means?" Noah asked.

"Yes."

Noah nodded. "I've been thinking about the good things we've got—things being 'copacetic.' I don't want to fall prey to 'not knowing what you've got till it's gone.' Community is another big one. I wonder if I could commute to Indiana, hold that job till something comes up around here—what are you staring at?" Noah asked.

"Look at that girl over there with the tray of drinks."

"Looks like root beer floats to me."

"Three root beer floats! She's obviously not drinking them by herself."

"So?"

"Well, that's what I was staring at," Eleanor explained. Both of them watched the girl as she set her tray of root beer floats on top of her Buick. "Now it looks like she's talking to someone. Do you see anyone, Noah?"

"She doesn't look old enough to drive. Maybe she's waiting for her parents."

Suddenly a car behind them honked. "Oh!" Noah waved out the truck window and advanced the vehicle forward in the queue. Their view of the lone girl became obscured by the building.

***

"We gotta' go!" Jonah yelled in a suppressed whisper.

Leslie set the root beer floats on top the car. "What are you doing crouched behind the car?"

"That's my parents over there in the drive-thru," Jonah said. "Don't look! Be secretive about it."

Leslie glanced out the corner of her eyes. "What are they driving?"

"'76 Chevy C30"

"70-30 what?"

"It's a white and yellow truck!" Jonah said in a suppressed shout.

"Oh, I think I saw the tail end; it's blocked by the building now."

Jonah carefully looked through the windows of Leslie's car, and from his angle, he could see the truck had gone behind the building. "What's taking Reinhardt so long? Leslie, fire up the car and be ready to peel outta' here." Jonah ran back inside the building.

Reinhardt had just come out of the restroom and was eyeing the spiraling descent of a gumball through a gumball machine.

"Reinhardt! Move your butt, we gotta' split!" Jonah practically pushed him out the door and all the way into Leslie's car. "Go, Leslie, go!" In all the excitement the root beer floats were completely forgotten on top of the car, and as Leslie careened into the street and floored it through a reddening traffic light, the root beer floats were sent halfway across the intersection in a dazzling display of soda, froth, and ice cream chunks.

"Shit!" Jonah bellowed.

"Oh my god!" Leslie screamed.

"I don't even have my seatbelt on," Reinhardt added.

"That light was yellow right?" Leslie asked; her voice was shaky and she was accelerating past the speed limit.

Jonah looked behind him. The distancing red traffic light was obscured by a different red light flashing in rhythm with blue. "Uh, I think it must have been pretty red," Jonah said.

***

Noah and Eleanor pulled out onto the street up to a red traffic light. Eleanor looked at the parlor's parking lot. "That girl must have found whoever she was looking for."

"Oh, someone got nailed," Noah remarked.

"What's that?"

"Down old 33, someone got pulled over. How about we take 29 home? I'd like to see if any farmers are out planting."

Eleanor licked the ice cream cone. "Okay, dear. Just watch that mess on the road," she said.

As Noah turned right, he said, "Maybe I should have gotten a root beer float."

***

"License and registration, Miss."

Leslie fumbled in her purse for her license and handed it to the officer.

"Registration, Miss." Leslie looked at him wide-eyed and clueless. "Check the glove box."

Jonah opened the glove box and pulled out all the papers, handing them to Leslie, who in turn handed the stack to the officer. From the stack he plucked a document. "You can put the rest away," he said, handing back the stack, which included the car manual.

"Leslie Schreiber," the Officer read off the license.

"Yes, Officer?" Her voice was thin and trembling.

"May I ask who your friends are?"

Leslie nodded, but didn't speak.

"I'm Jonah, Sir. This is my little brother Reinhardt. Brandtmeyers, Sir."

The officer looked to each boy in turn through his dark aviators. His movements were jerky. "Brandtmeyer. Interesting."

He turned his attention back to Leslie. "Do you know why I pulled you over?" She shook her head. "Tell me, Miss Schreiber, did you pass driving school by running red lights?" His aviator sunglasses and lack of vocal inflection made his voice quite intimidating. Leslie just shook her head. "Tell me, Miss Schreiber, in the few hours you have been driving, has it been your habit to place things on top your car then push the speed limit to its breaking point to see if they stay on top?"

Tears streamed down Leslie's face, washing mascara down her cheeks. The officer procured a tissue from his utility belt and offered it to Leslie. "Thankfully for you, Miss Schreiber, this isn't my first rodeo. Hold on, please." The officer returned to his squad car.

"This 'ain't' my first rodeo," Jonah said. "Man, does this guy have a stick up his butt or what?" No one responded. Leslie snuffled in her tissue, and Reinhardt snuck glances out the back window. Jonah shuffled his feet on the floor boards and did not say anything else.

The officer was in his car a long while. Presently, a sheriff's car pulled up. The original officer strode back to Leslie's car. "Do you boys know Marilla Brandtmeyer?"

"She's our grandma."

"She gave permission for your county's sheriff to escort you Brandtmeyer boys home." At this remark, Jonah let out a defeated groan; his head collapsed into the palms of his hands.

The boys were introduced to Sheriff Deputy Ransburg. He was not wearing sunglasses. His brimmed hat with a six-pointed gold star on the front looked impressive. His smile was inviting.

"Come along, boys. Let's get you home," he said.

"Will Leslie be alright?" Jonah asked as he ducked into the deputy sheriff's car. No one, other than Reinhardt, heard his question. Through the front windshield, the boys watched the deputy and police officer talking about something. From their position in the backseat, they could not see whether or not Leslie had stopped crying.

***

Deputy Ransburg drove his car up the lane and stopped at the windbreak where Captain began his barking campaign.

"Oh no," muttered Jonah. From across the backyard, he saw Grandma swinging a stick to fend off a rogue group of rooting piglets from the garden. The white and yellow Chevy was parked in a manner to block off the lane that ran to the woods. Both his parents had sorting panels in hand and with much success were corralling the escaped Berkshires into the backside of the farrowing barn.

"Deputy Ransburg, may we jump out here and help?" Jonah asked.

"Ol' Captain here, he won't bother you," explained Reinhardt. "That's the dog."

"You're not being detained."

Jonah ran straight for the farrowing barn's front door. Inside, the twine-tied stall door was wrenched open; an obvious path of little pig trotters marked the ground. He discarded the twine evidence and frantically started jamming and jostling the latch. From the back, pigs were returning accompanied by the calls of "Suey!" "Haw!" and "Giddyup!" Jonah broke into a cold sweat, and after several loud jerks, the latch locked into the closed position. He leaned against the gate, let out a sigh, and shook his head. "Unbelievable, stupid gate, stupid twine, stupid pigs. Ruin everything." His feet dragged as he went back outside.

"Where in the world were you!?" Noah's face was covered in perspiration and disbelief.

Reinhardt stood by his mother wringing his hands and chewing on his lips. Jonah was leaning with his back against the barn wall, his head turned down, but his eyes strained towards his father. Noah looked to his wife and was shaking his head; he rubbed the back of his neck. Deputy Ransburg pulled his car into the yard.

"Hello folks." He stepped out. "I'm Deputy Ransburg."

Noah shook his hand and introduced himself and his wife. "What did my boys do?"

"No worries. Your boys aren't in any trouble with the law, but to answer your question they were in Saint Marys, joyriding with a girl who got pulled over."

"Leslie," Jonah said.

"And you boys left Grandma alone?" Noah asked in a stern tone. "And you didn't even tell her you were leaving? She was told by the police!"

"Is this the girl that just got her license?" Eleanor asked.

Jonah shifted his weight from leg to leg. Reinhardt had a clueless look on his face and stared at his big brother for answers.

"Even more irresponsible!" Noah said, "I'm guessing the pigs escaped because of your carelessness? Why did you run inside the farrowing barn?"

Jonah nodded and muttered something unintelligible.

"What?"

Jonah said audibly, "I said, 'if it weren't for the finicky latch...'"

"You know the latch is finicky, so why didn't you make sure it was secure? Anything worth doing is—"

"—is worth doing right, Dad, I know."

"Don't cut me off."

"Noah," said Eleanor.

Jonah said, "Granddad taught me that. Just like most everything else. Then you go selling his Wood-Mizer."

"Son, I told you to drop it. It wasn't even paid off."

"Whose fault is that?"

"Your granddad's, but he isn't here anymore is he!?" Noah's voice was rising.

Jonah shot back, "Well, sometimes I wish I was with him instead!"

It was silent in the barnyard for a moment. Grandma, who had been quietly observing the situation, broke the silence blowing her nose. Eleanor walked over to her; everyone became aware she was crying.

"Come with me boys," Noah said. He waved them to follow. "Good day, Deputy." Noah nodded a farewell. "Eleanor please see Deputy, uh…"

"Ransburg."

"Ransburg out, and thank you again for bringing my sons home safely."

"My pleasure, Mr. Brandtmeyer."

Noah and his sons entered the farmhouse. In the mudroom, he handed Reinhardt a broom; to Jonah he gave a mop and bucket filled with a box of soap, window cleaner, and rags. Noah grabbed a large garbage can.

"Come along," he said. With their equipment in hand, Noah led them out the door and back across the farmyard. Eleanor and Grandma sat on the porch swing; his wife was still speaking with Deputy Ransburg. Noah and the boys walked past the barns, past the water gauge, past the orchard, down the east lane, to the Quonset. Noah led them to the shop side and set the garbage can down by the door. "Here, if you want to be with your granddad this is the best I can do. While you're here, you can clean this place up." He opened the door and surveyed the surroundings. "I'll be back later, and it better look shaped up in here."

***

Returning to the farmyard, Noah found Deputy Ransburg still there, along with two more men in dark coats sitting on his porch swing. Eleanor just finished serving them coffee.

"Mr. Brandtmeyer," Ransburg began, "this is Detective Emerson and Detective Irving."

Noah stood dumbfounded.

"We won't take too much of your time, Mr. Brandtmeyer," Detective Emerson began.

The other turned to Ransburg. "Thank you, Deputy, for the introduction." The detectives stood quietly staring at him.

"Oh, right," Ransburg said. "Farewell, Brandtmeyers. It was nice meeting you." He shook their hands. Irving walked the deputy to his car, made a few inaudible parting remarks, then grabbed a briefcase from his own vehicle.

Detective Emerson waited for Irving to rejoin them on the porch and then addressed Noah. "We have a few questions we would like answers to regarding your recent contact with Albrecht Katterheinrich."

"Oh," Noah exhaled, "sorry maybe you've got the wrong guy." He had been holding his breath. "I don't know anyone by that name."

Detective Irving proffered a small recording device from his briefcase and played back Noah's message he left on "Heinrich's" answering machine. "It appears you do, Mr. Brandtmeyer, and it would go well with you to cooperate."

"Noah," Eleanor's voice was shaky, "what's this all about?"

"Settle down, settle down everyone." Noah's hands rose in defense. "I can explain. That was nothing. I didn't know his name was Albrecht. I bumped into a man last week who introduced himself as Al. The message on the machine testifies to that." He nodded to the detectives. "I'm in a lot of debt, farm debt, good honest farm debt, nothing else. Al offered me a side job. The message explains I didn't take it."

"We believe you, Mr. Brandtmeyer," Emerson said. "We checked your background—you're clean as the driven snow. Take a breath, you look pale—no one is accusing you. We would like to know how Albrecht, or Al as you know him, came to offer you a job. Could you tell us about that?"

"As I said, I met him last week..."

"What day?"

.

"Friday. At Traders Co. It's a pawn shop in Saint Marys—big red sign with a steam engine, can't miss it," Noah explained.

"And you just bumped into Al? Why were you there?"

Noah looked at his wife then continued, "I asked if they were in the business of buying stuff."

"This was Al you asked? Al was working there?"

"Not exactly. I'm not explaining this very well."

"Just take a deep breath and tell us like it happened, like you were telling your—" Emerson had been looking to Eleanor, but suddenly averted his gaze, "like you were telling the story to your dog."

Noah sat on the porch steps. "Eleanor, could you get me a coffee as well, please?"

With rigid movements, Eleanor stepped inside the house.

"I'm a little embarrassed. I didn't tell my wife I was planning on selling anything," Noah explained. "When I asked about this the lady asked for my I.D. She went down a flight of stairs and was gone five minutes, and when she returned instructed me to go down the stairs. Downstairs is where I made my acquaintance with Al. He was working on a model train, we spoke, and he took a liking to me. He offered me work and said he'd reach out to me for details."

Eleanor returned to the porch; she handed Noah the coffee. He took a sip.

"Then he reached out to you?" Emerson asked.

"Thanks for the coffee, Eleanor." Noah said, "And sorry I didn't tell you all this." He turned his attention back to Emerson. "Yeah, he sent a man here Saturday morning with a note and phone number to the place where I left the message." He brought out the slip of paper from his wallet and handed it to Emerson. From the corner of his eye, he saw Eleanor frowning with arms crossed.

Emerson looked to Irving. Both reviewed the note. Irving leaned in and whispered something in Emerson's ear.

"Right," Emerson said. "You said Al was working on a model train, and I'm picturing a basement. Can you tell us more about that?"

Noah explained the room, the traders' guild, and the office space.

"Did it appear to you this was Al's office?"

"Yes, definitely," Noah confirmed.

"And not just a random space he was working in? How can you know?"

Noah rubbed his chin in thought. "That's a good question. I had only assumed but, two reasons: he had on display some sort of device, 'Panzerfäust' he called it. He was proud of this item, I could tell—but then again, maybe it wasn't his? However, there was a filing cabinet and he had the key to the cabinet attached to a ring of keys on his belt."

"Good work, Mr. Brandtmeyer, good work," Emerson encouraged. "Now tell us what you know regarding 'Operation Panzerfäust.'"

Noah thought a moment. "He never mentioned it to me in our conversation. He only asked me to deliver something for him. I assumed 'Operation Panzerfäust' was his way of communicating that to me in a note."

"Now you declined the job, and reason stands Al still needs a man. Would it be possible to suggest a friend for the job?" Emerson asked. Irving had been taking notes up to this point, but stopped and put an arm on Emerson's shoulder.

"Not that way," Irving said to Emerson. Then he addressed Noah, "A moment ago you said Al 'took a liking' to you. Why do you think that was?"

"Well honestly, I think it's because of my German heritage."

Irving nodded thoughtfully. "Interesting." He handed Emerson the notepad, "Take notes, Emerson. Go on, Noah." There was a gleam in Irving's eye. "Tell us more about your time spent with Albrecht."

Noah shrugged. "Well, he was proud of the 'Fatherland' as he put it, offered me a cigarette, and our conversation circled back to selling heirlooms. He had a Nazi artifact, said they fetched high prices. He asked if that was the nature of what I wanted to sell, of course it wasn't. Again, I didn't actually have anything to sell." Noah finished with a glance at Eleanor.

"There we have it, Emerson," Irving said with a smile. "Have H.Q. scrounge up some 3rd Reich memorabilia. We send in one of our guys looking for a sympathetic buyer," he clenched his fist, "and the noose tightens."

Emerson nodded in agreement. "Brilliant, Sir." Then he looked to Noah. "Mind if I hold on to the note you received, Mr. Brandtmeyer?"

"It's all yours," Noah said. "Though do I have a choice?"

"No." Irving winked. "It's being confiscated as evidence, but we like to come across as congenial to those who cooperate."

Emerson stashed the slip of paper along with their other notes into the briefcase. The men stood up to leave.

"That's it?" Noah asked.

"That's it," Emerson said. "Thank you, Eleanor for the cup o' Joe." He and Irving set their mugs on the porch rail. They shook hands with the Brandtmeyers and headed to their car.

"One last thing, Mr. and Mrs. Brandtmeyer," Irving turned and said, "I trust you're not going back to that shop? You would be hindering an investigation. Am I understood?"

"Yes, Detective. We won't be going back there," Noah assured. "And Heinrich's too?"

Irving, hand on the car latch, paused in thought. Emerson, about to enter the passenger's seat looked for Irving's cue.

"On second thought, you drive, Emerson," Irving said and tossed him the keys. Irving walked back to Noah and stood very close. He spoke slowly, "Mr. Brandtmeyer, let the record show, I never infringed on your freedoms. May I encourage you to cultivate an appetite for something other than bratwurst?" Without another word the detectives left.

Noah and his wife stood on the porch and watched the men leave. Then Eleanor turned on Noah with an icy expression, and he had to retell his conversation with Al all over again.

"And what do we have that you intended to pawn?" Eleanor asked.

"I mean..." Noah stammered. "You heard in the message I left—that I didn't actually have anything."

"Hmm," she let the matter pass, "but you very well may have been stumbling headlong into disaster. We've managed to stay afloat, and we've always made decisions together. Let's keep it that way."

Noah collapsed into the swing and was frowning.

"Let's keep it that way. Right?" Eleanor reiterated.

"Yes, Eleanor!" He barked. "I don't need you reprimanding me. Listen, I'm just trying different things. You know I didn't want to sell Dad's Wood-Mizer. Look at the storm that's made with Jonah. When this opportunity with Al came up, how was I supposed to know strings would be attached?"

Eleanor did not respond, but after a moment sat down next to her husband on the swing. Both were quiet for a minute and looked out across the lawn.

"Is Mother alright?" Noah asked.

"She's alright—went in for a nap." Eleanor sighed. "I understand you're looking for opportunities. I didn't mean it like that, and I think selling the Wood-Mizer was the right thing to do."

"How are you doing?"

Eleanor shook her head. "Still a bit shaken both our sons ran off without telling us. That's a first."

"And not the last time, I'm sure," Noah mused. "I'll call Mr. Schreiber—let him know what his daughter was up to today."

"Speaking of which, what are the boys up to?"

***

"That could have gone worse," Reinhardt said.

"It's not over yet," Jonah said. "Cleaning up is hardly a punishment."

"And the Frostop is still on the shelf."

"Now we can really find the bottle opener."

"How should we go about cleaning?" Reinhardt asked.

"You hit the cobwebs; I'll start chucking all those bottles in the can."

"Are you still angry with Dad?"

"About the Wood-Mizer? Obviously. Not only was that a piece of Granddad, but I could have made that my business, in another year and a half, get my license, tow that sawmill around, make some cash, be my own boss. That's all gone. A labor for hire is all I can hope to be now."

Reinhardt wrinkled his forehead. "Why would you do that? We work here all the time."

"I don't know if you noticed Reinhardt, but there isn't any money here. Mom and Dad can't afford to pay us for our help."

Reinhardt swirled some cobwebs. "Money for what?"

"Well gee, I don't know Reinhardt? Ice cream, cotton candy?" Jonah cooled his sarcasm and continued, "A car for one, or better yet, a truck."

"I thought you wanted a mo-ped?"

"It's too late for that. After seeing Leslie's car—sixteen isn't too far off. Dad says I could probably find paid work on another farm."

They both cleaned. Hours of spiderweb spinning were destroyed in seconds with the careless swooping of Reinhardt's broom. Jonah lobbed glass bottles into the trash can, some shattering on impact. It didn't take long for the entire bin to be filled.

Jonah said, "Maybe I should smash the rest to fit more." He took the shovel from the corner and spent a few minutes obliterating all the bottles that were in the trash.

"Let me try." Reinhardt ground the glass to smithereens. Next, they worked on clearing the floor and carried the couch outside.

"Slow, Jonah. It's heavy."

"Don't be so weak," but Jonah was smiling as they lumbered out the door. "Here just drop it. It's not a prized piece of carpentry."

They piled the boxes into a semi-orderly heap against the bare wall opposite the book shelf, swept the whole place down, and mopped the floor.

"We'll let the floors dry before we put this back inside," Jonah said as he dropped onto the couch.

His little brother asked, "Should we have carried all the boxes out here too and then mopped the floor?"

"That ship sailed about an hour ago, Reinhardt."

Reinhardt joined Jonah on the couch. An audible bump came from underneath as an object dislodged from the old piece of furniture. Reinhardt slipped back off and looked under the couch.

"Hey look!" He held up a bottle opener.

"So, it was in the couch after all. Just needed roughed up a bit."

Together they sat on the couch drinking their Frostop. "I don't mind it warm," said Reinhardt.

"Me neither, sometimes I like it this way. I think it's sweeter."

"Maybe we'll find that missing journal of Granddad's."

"Hmm, Journal '86, if there ever was one. I've looked all around. Whatever clues it held disappeared with him."

Reinhardt thought and added hopefully, "We found the bottle opener. That's something."

"Genius, Reinhardt, that's the clue. No doubt Granddad ran off to the Frostop factory."

The sun was getting well on in the sky.

"Do you think if Dad returns right now, and sees us lying around, he will get mad?" asked Reinhardt.

"No, he shouldn't anyways; we really did spruce the place up. We'll tell him we were just about to finish dusting and cleaning the windows."

When Noah did return, he called Reinhardt to walk with him. "Let's walk and talk. Jonah, don't forget to dust the bookshelf and desk while you're at it."

Reinhardt and his father took to the lane. "Tell me a little more about today," Noah said. Reinhardt told his father about helping Grandma, the search for morels, and then the girl showing up. "Had you met her before?"

"I recognized her from the festival; she was with Jonah. Jonah knows her really."

"Whose idea was it to leave?"

"The girl's."

"Why didn't you tell Grandma your plans?"

"I was going to, but Jonah wanted me to hurry up."

Noah nodded. "Yes, that's what I wanted to point out to you. Listen, you don't need to follow your brother's orders especially if your gut tells you otherwise. You're old enough now to make some judgements on your own that may be contrary to that of your brother's. Do you understand?"

"I think so."

"If he has an idea, but that idea worries you —talk to me first or in this case Grandma. If for some reason you can't reach any of us, Pastor John is another great and reliable adult to reach out to."

"But what if there isn't time?"

"Time to ask?"

"Yeah."

"If your brother is creating a sense that the situation does not allow time for good decision making, that should be your first clue."

Reinhardt nodded. "I see. I understand. That's what happened today. Sorry, Dad."

"I forgive you, son." Noah gave him a hug. "Oh, and one last thing. Who paid for the ice cream?"

"Jonah."

"I see," Noah said. "Thanks, Reinhardt. Now run on up to the house and tell your mother and grandmother you're sorry. Your poor mother is a little shaken to know both her boys ran off today."

As Reinhardt began to run, Noah called out, "Oh, and Reinhardt! I love you, son."

"I love you too, Dad."

8

THE CHEVY rumbled to life. The noise woke Jonah who had been asleep upstairs. Weathered floorboards creaked under his footsteps as he went to the window. The Chevy reached the end of the lane and turned north. Jonah's breath fogged the windowpane as he watched the truck disappear down the road.

After dressing, he went downstairs. He found his mother shuffling around in the kitchen. The scent of coffee and toast was in the air.

"Where'd Dad go?"

"Good morning, Jonah, your father had to run errands this morning."

"When will he be back?"

"I'm not sure, but he left a list on the fridge for you and Reinhardt."

Jonah read through the list. It covered the basics with a few other odds and ends—"unload circus wagon"—things of that nature that always needed done, but never would be *done* for all eternity, like stocking the firewood supply.

"This is great," he said under his breath.

"What? Is something wrong?"

"It's nothing."

Eleanor frowned. She set her coffee mug on the counter and came to give her son a hug. "You know son, I used to have to crouch down to hug you, but you've grown so big. You're taller than me." She smiled at him. "Listen Jonah, your father and I love you very much—don't roll your eyes."

"Okay Mom," he said as he took a step back. He was looking down and rubbing his forehead. "Well, I've got things to do." He waved the list. A piece of toast protruded from the toaster. Jonah grabbed it. "Can I have this?"

"Yes, but come back for lunch. I'll make sandwiches."

Jonah held the toast in his mouth, stuffed the list in his front pocket, slipped on his work boots, and went outside. "And we need to do school later!" she called out the door.

"Okay Mom, I'll be around. Send Reinhardt out when he wakes up."

Late in the morning, Reinhardt came out and found Jonah at the farrowing barn. He asked his older brother, "Did Mom tell you where Dad went?"

"No," Jonah said. "I'm glad he's not around. I didn't want to see him."

"Why?" Reinhardt asked with a shrug. "You said yourself, 'cleaning is hardly a punishment.'"

Jonah's eyes narrowed in suspicion and he stared fixedly at his little brother with a curious expression.

"I just thought Mom was weird about it when I asked her," Reinhardt explained.

"Did you check the chickens already?"

"No, I just came out."

"Well do that. I'll finish up here then meet me behind the house."

"What's back there?" Reinhardt asked.

"Those logs from the woods."

Reinhardt stared blank faced.

"The logs in the circus wagon!" Jonah said irritated. "Sheesh, Rein—" he caught his breath, "just go."

"Oh, those logs, right."

Once Reinhardt had finished tending the hens and brought in the eggs, he joined Jonah behind the house. On the back of the house there was a small hatch for tossing logs down into the basement. In the winter the furnace would be lit and stoked. Last season Reinhardt had lost many games of *rock-paper-scissors* and had been the one to stoke the furnace.

"It's pretty empty down there. Let's chuck them all down first and then stack them together."

"Okay," Reinhardt said.

Once the wagon was emptied, Reinhardt asked, "Can I fetch the tractor? I've been practicing hitching up."

Jonah's eyes widened in wonder, "Really? Sure, go ahead." Reinhardt brought the tractor around, and Jonah closed up the basement hatch.

Jonah called out over the putter of the tractor's engine, "Just don't pin me between the tractor and the wagon please." Reinhardt smiled, and then with several jerks and clutch grinds, he maneuvered the tractor into an acceptable position.

"Well, not too bad little brother, but only because the wagon is empty and light enough to rock. Here, hold the tongue and hitch pin; I'll rock it for you." Jonah heave-hoed the wagon into alignment, and Reinhardt dropped the hitch pin through the holes.

"Thanks, Jonah. Practice," Reinhardt said, "makes one better."

"That it does. Can you take this to the shed and back it in?"

Reinhardt cringed. "Well, I'm likely to jackknife it."

Jonah nodded. "Yeah, me too," and he took the driver's seat, shuffled a bit on the hard surface of the seat, then stood back up. Reinhardt was standing on the hitch pin aloof and smiling; Jonah eyed his little brother with the same curious expression he had earlier.

"What?" Reinhardt said when he saw his brother's look.

Jonah responded more to himself, "Still a little sore." Then he said, "Why don't you drive, Reinhardt? We'll just pull it into the barnyard."

Reinhardt parked it in front of the shed. He hopped off the tractor seat, and his mood was good. Jonah continued eyeing his brother and asked, "Isn't it especially uncomfortable in that hard seat?"

"Not particularly," Reinhardt said.

"I'll make it hurt!" Jonah side-stepped at the same time and gave Reinhardt a side-wind kick square on the backside. It knocked Reinhardt down.

"Jonah, why!?" Reinhardt croaked as he slowly maneuvered away from his brother on hands and knees.

"Dad didn't give you the belt?"

"Huh? What are you talking about?"

"Yesterday?"

"No, he gave you one?"

"Unbelievable!" Jonah shoved Reinhardt and began to walk away. Just then they heard their mother called out from the porch.

"Boys, I've got lunch—" Her voice broke off seeing them close at hand and Reinhardt laying in the gravel. "Jonah, what did you do to your brother!?" She came down the porch steps, but didn't have any shoes on. "Come inside this instant, both of you." Reinhardt quickly ran with his head dipping down between his shoulders and stealing glances behind him. Jonah kept his distance coming up at a slow walk. Eleanor took Reinhardt inside and sent him to the bathroom to wash up. She came back to a sulking son in the mudroom. "Reinhardt tells me you kicked him? What on earth did you do that for?"

Jonah didn't respond.

"Go to the table, and when Reinhardt joins us, you apologize. Do you hear me?"

"Alright, Mom."

"Go."

At the table Jonah picked at his food. "Are you going to tell Dad?" he asked.

Eleanor said, "If you resolve this with your brother you won't need to be concerned."

"Well, when is Dad getting home?"

"He hasn't called yet to let me know."

"Where did he go?"

Eleanor, standing at the kitchen sink, had her back to him and spoke slowly, "I believe your father wanted to talk to you yesterday about that, but the day went a little south. I think it would be best if you waited until he returns. After all, it may come to nothing."

"What may come to nothing?"

Reinhardt had crept to the kitchen doorway. He asked, "Did Dad go back to Indiana?"

Eleanor turned from her distraction at the sink and faced her sons. "How did you know that?"

"I didn't know. I was asking," Reinhardt said.

Jonah's mood grew darker.

"Son—"

"He's taking a job in Indiana!?" Jonah yelled.

"It may come to nothing; it's just an inter—"

"I'm not moving to Indiana, Mom!" Jonah yelled as he jumped up and knocked his chair back. "I'm not moving there!" He declared again as he stomped to the front door.

"Where are you going? Jonah. Jonah, come back inside and be reasonable," Eleanor pleaded following after him.

Jonah slammed the door on his way out, leaving his mother exasperated. She came back to the kitchen and wiped her face on the towel and leaned over the sink. Reinhardt picked up the chair that had toppled over, and then quietly slipped into his own seat at the table. He listened; Eleanor was breathing pretty regularly.

"Mom, are we leaving the farm?"

9

JONAH flung the door of the old shop office open. The photo of Grandad and his Wood-Mizer fell off the wall without shattering—since the glass was already broken out. He glared at it; he glared around the room. It was tidy. He pounded his fist against the bookshelf.

"Where are you, Granddad!? Where have you gone? Why did you go?" He yelled at the line of journals and shoved them into the back of the shelf. Then he threw the desk chair to the floor, and with the last flare of anger, he turned the entire desk over.

The heavy oak desk made a thunderous crash into the cement floor. The top drawer bounced up spilling pencils, pliers, papers, screwdrivers, and scissors. A side panel split off the frame revealing the internal empty space behind the drawers. In the dead space a book was caught.

Angry tears clung to Jonah's eyes blurring his vision as he stared. But the book held his attention. He rubbed the tears away with the back of his hand. Slowly he crouched down by the book, slower still he reached out and pulled it from the dead space. He had held many others like it. He turned the binding to face him; on its hard blue surface, etched in gold, was the number '86. Clutching the book to his chest, he collapsed onto the couch.

He flipped to the final entry which came early on within the pages; a quick thumb through revealed all the rest after to be blank. The entry was simply the date: "May 6, 1986 and a list: "Lantern, matches, pick-adze, rope, canteen, shovel, compass, watch, pack—jerky, jacket, &c."

Jonah flipped to the preceding entry: "May 4, 1986. Great pie, God bless her. We did have to hold the picnic in the church basement though. Lots of talk about that—rain in torrents. Everyone's chomping at the bit to get crops in. Pastor John's sermon from Matthew (treasure in field). Must confess made me think of the spot in the woods the whole sermon. Dark and rainy all day—perhaps in a day or two if the rain subsides."

And the previous entry: "May 3, 1986. Three inches of rain. Marilla baking all day in summer kitchen. Went walking during a lull in the rain. Due E. of sinkhole, all the way to the woods Eastern quarter where the shift in elevation is so sudden and sharp, I saw a small amount of water trickling out of the "seam" between the flat land and the shift. Above the higher ground, I saw the top of a fallen oak. It must have fallen this winter, but being so dense—and steep—I couldn't get up to the oak. I took a wide berth northward around the area and came out of the woods on the eastern side, then following the edge south, I discovered an opening into the dense thicket. I've never trekked this spot of the woods before.

"At the fallen oak, I discovered a large stash of morels making this spot a gem in the rough... When the going gets tough there's the gem in the rough! Head to the east, and find these sneaky little beasts! Anyways, happy with my discovery of the morels, I was about to leave when something caught my eye.

"At the base of the fallen oak, where the enormous root bulb had ripped the earth, I noticed the *lack* of water pooling—absolutely no water filling the crater. The falling of the tree also appeared to have shifted some rather large rocks. The whole spot appeared to be one big drain. I suppose the water trickling out of that seam below is fed from here. The rain picked up again, and little streams flowed into the divot disappearing between the rocks. It began coming down in torrents as soon as I reached the Quonset."

At the end of the entry, there was a sketch of the wooded area.

The prior journal entry: April 30, 1986 had a brief timetable of planting dates, weather conditions, and forecast.

"Holy crap, Granddad, what did you find?" Jonah said aloud to himself. He re-read the entries once more, this time chronologically.

Jonah closed the journal. He pulled his to-do list from his pocket, and fetching a pencil from the floor, he wrote: Backpack, canteen, lantern, flashlight, rope. He re-opened Granddad's journal and drew his finger down the page. On his scrap he finished: "Matches, compass, watch." He circled the word *watch* and chewed on the end of his pencil. "Don't have one of those," he muttered, "and what's a pick-*adze*?" He looked to where they had organized the tools from the day before. "There's a pick-*axe*..." Jonah's face, red from crying, smiled a little. "*Adze*," he said the word slowly. "I always thought he was saying *axe*." Jonah touched the handle of the tool: one end had a pick and the other end had a horizontal blade designed for digging and hoeing.

He tucked the list in the front pocket of his flannel and set Journal '86 on the shelf. His hand hesitated on the book. "I'll be back," he said to the journal.

Jonah returned to the farmyard. A racing heart and shaky hands ailed him, and though anxious, he was careful to tend to the animals without mishap. While going from barn to shed, he looked for the items on his list. All he found was a coil of rope which he stashed just inside the farrowing barn door. Jonah frowned and reassessed the list. He looked to the house, swallowed, and straightened up.

***

"Sorry, Mom, for my attitude."

"I forgive you." Eleanor stood still, staring at him. Her silence forced him to continue.

"Where is Reinhardt?"

"He's in the basement. I was just going down there myself. I'll join you." Eleanor went first. They descended the old creaky basement steps. There was a deep freezer in the basement that Eleanor went to in view of where the logs were being stacked. She watched Jonah closely.

Reinhardt looked up from where he stacked the logs.

"I really am sorry for earlier, Reinhardt. It's just... it shocked me in the moment, and seemed unfair. But either way, I got over it."

"I forgive you, and I don't know why Dad gave you the belt but not me."

"Let's just forget about it. Okay?"

Reinhardt nodded. "Look, I got most of this stacked." He pointed to the logs and offered a smile.

"Thanks, good job."

Mom went back upstairs empty handed, and together the boys finished the stacking.

"Hey, listen," Jonah said, dusting his hands off on his pant legs, "we've pretty much finished our chores. I think we have time to look for morels again, and maybe do a little exploring in the woods."

"Okay. Is the list really done?"

"Pretty much, there are a few things that need gathered up, and taken to the Quonset, but we can do that on the way."

"Okay, I'm down."

Returning up the creaking stairs, their mother called from another room in the house, "How you boys doing?"

"We're good, Mom! We're going to—uhfu—"

Jonah had shot out an arm to silence him. "We're going to head outside for a bit," then he whispered to Reinhardt, "I thought the morels should be a surprise if we actually find some."

"Oh, gotcha'." Reinhardt gave a thumbs-up.

Then Jonah continued in a loud voice speaking to his mother, "May I have that sandwich? I'll take it with me."

"Okay."

"And wrap it up, please?" He fished the list out of his front pocket and said to Reinhardt, "I'm going to grab my backpack from upstairs, can you get the sandwich, oh, and also let's take some jerky if there is any, and fill a canteen of water for us too, okay?"

Upstairs, Jonah filled his backpack: a compass from his nightstand drawer and from the closet a small battery powered lantern used for camping—a quick flip of the switch showed it still had battery power. When Jonah returned downstairs, Reinhardt was in the mudroom putting on his boots. The food supplies sat next to him on the bench; there was a nice supply of pork jerky too. All this, plus matches and two more flashlights from the mudroom shelf were stowed in Jonah's backpack.

Reinhardt asked, "Are we camping?"

"Huh?"

"What's with all the stuff?"

"I just want some stuff, and that reminds me there are a few things, some here and some outside, some stuff that needs taken to the woods. But you can help me since we're headed that way." Jonah had a matter-of-fact expression and was looking around the small room. He grabbed a jacket from a peg and stuffed it in his pack as well. "I don't know? It's been unseasonably warm. You know, Reinhardt, I think we will find some morels today."

Reinhardt just smiled, and together they went outside. Jonah grabbed the coil of rope from inside the farrowing barn and took one last glance at the pigs. "Thanks for the jerky," he said and waved farewell. Down the lane to the Quonset, the brothers went.

10

"WAIT HERE, I just need to grab the pick-adze." Inside the shop office Jonah smuggled the journal into his pack. Eyeing the broken desk, he cringed, grabbed the pick-adze, then checking his list, gave a nod and departed.

"We need the pick-axe to find morels?"

"Pffft, pick-*adze*, Reinhardt, A-D-Z-E," Jonah scoffed. He looked to the horizon and the sun, with right arm outstretched and palm facing him, he estimated the remaining daylight. "Hmm, less than an hour," he said under his breath.

"What?"

"Yes, Reinhardt, we need the pick-adze to find the morels. Come on, we're headed east."

They entered through the gate they had repaired that Friday. Following a pig trail, they walked east. Passing by the sink hole, Reinhardt asked, "Shouldn't we search around this spot? They've been here before."

"Not today, it's still too early in the season. Today we head far far east into the woods."

Soon the pig trail meandered south. Jonah retrieved his compass from his backpack and reset their course. With the woodland foliage still new, it was a tame trek. Eventually they approached a shift in the ground. This formed a steep cliff-like bank which blocked their course. Above the bank a very overgrown, thick tangled mess of thickets grew. Jonah stooped at the base of the bank and observed erosion among the rock. The earth at his feet was damp, and the pale purple blossoms of Waterleaf speckled about.

"Reinhardt, hand me that pick-adze." Jonah slipped the pack off and set it against the wall of the cliff. With pick-adze in hand Jonah explored, jarring a few rocks around with the pick of the tool.

"Jonah, morels don't grow in the rocks."

"Right," Jonah confirmed, "can you shoulder the pack for a little?"

Reinhardt set the rope down and shouldered the pack. "Let me check something," Jonah said. He set the pick-adze next to the rope. While Reinhardt had the pack on, Jonah rummaged inside and pulled out the journal. He opened to Granddad's sketch. "Reinhardt, look at this spot here." Jonah brought the map into his view. "Do you see—?"

"Wow! Is that a real map!?" Reinhardt broke in.

"Yes, it's a map—"

"That's in one of Granddad's journals? Which one? I never saw a map, and you never mentioned one."

"Yes, I know. I'd forgotten," Jonah said. "It's a map to morels. Now look here, would you say this spot is where we are?"

Reinhardt reached out to take the map in hand, but Jonah pulled it away.

Jonah continued, "Look, I think this is where we are."

"May I see, please?"

"Yeah, in a minute, look here." Jonah pointed at the erosion among the rocks. "Does it look like water has eroded this spot?

But see how it's not from above, there isn't a path coming down, but it starts around this rocky area."

"I see. What does that mean?"

"I think it means, probably when there are heavy rains, water comes out of the ground here along the base of this ridge—but apparently not all the time. And see this Waterleaf? My guess is during a lot of rain it flows out—just a trickle, but enough to keep the Waterleaf happy."

"What does that mean for us?"

"I'm just curious if the spot fits the bill," Jonah said, rubbing his chin, "and I think so. Look at this bank; it's practically a cliff. Do you think we could climb this?"

Reinhardt looked up and down the bank that stretched in both directions. To the north it curved gently out of sight. He looked directly in front of them. "Maybe with the rope here, if we had a grappling hook, see that area of dead branches?" Reinhardt pointed slightly to the left. "Over those thickets, there's the top of a fallen tree, but we will get caught in the brambles. Maybe we could go farther around the north side there," he said, pointing where it curved out of sight. "Does the map want us to go over this?"

"That does look like the top of a fallen tree," Jonah agreed. "Let's follow this around the north, I expect it will curve eastward until we come out along the east border of the woods." He slipped the journal back into the pack; he had not let Reinhardt take a closer look. "I'll carry the pick and rope for a while. Let's go."

Following the bank, they found it curved east. Several spots of decaying wood hinted at the prospect of morels. "Is this the spot?" Reinhardt asked more than once.

"We're getting close to the grand prize," Jonah reassured. "We aren't looking for some little morel here or there, but the big stash. Let's keep going."

"Okay, if you say so." Reinhardt followed his brother, but continued to look over his shoulder at spots that caught the morel-hunter's eye. "We're losing daylight too, Jonah."

"We're nearly there, Reinhardt, have some patience."

"Don't blame me, it's the sun. It's practically set."

As Reinhardt was saying this, they stepped out from the tree line. The east horizon was quite dark by this hour, and with the remaining sunlight on the other side of the woods, the area was all in shadow.

"Damn, it is getting dark fast," Jonah admitted. "Hold still, Reinhardt." He rummaged in the pack on his little brothers back and pulled out a flashlight. He switched on the light, but it was not dark enough to make the flashlight useful. "Getting darker, but not dark, Reinhardt, come on. The morels are going to be along this edge if we head south now. Keep looking for an opening in the thickets."

Jonah quickened his pace with a renewed pep in his step. Reinhardt loosened the pack and trudged behind. And the distance between them grew.

Suddenly Jonah turned into the woods and became lost to Reinhardt's sight. "Jonah! Wait!" Reinhardt jogged up to the spot where he lost him; the pack bounced and jostled on his shoulders. Jonah reappeared from a small opening in the tangle of brush and vine. "Keep up, Reinhardt, geez, stop freaking out."

"I'm getting tired."

"I just found the spot and you want to quit?"

"You found the morels? Where?" He was peering at the ground around Jonah's feet as he asked.

Jonah turned back into the thickening shadows of the dense growth. "I found where they will be, just beyond these brambles."

Reinhardt took a step back, he shook his head, and fumbled his words, "I don't think, I feel like there, that we shouldn't go back into the woods now. It's gotten so dark…"

The older brother wheeled around. "Fine, Reiner, just go home!" In a swift fury, Jonah dropped the rope and pick-adze and snagged the pack from his little brother. "I'll get, I'll…" he trailed off as he foisted the pack on his shoulders. "Don't you dare tell Dad!" he finally yelled as he stomped off into the dark.

"Oh, come on, Jonah! Let's come back in the morning."

Jonah disappeared among the thickets, becoming lost in the dark. "Jonah, don't leave me here! And you left the rope!" He looked around. A star was visible on the horizon. Several minutes passed. "I wish I had a watch on," Reinhardt said looking at his wrist. In a more collected voice, he spoke loudly, "Jonah, if we head back now there will still be some light in the west… make it easier to get home… we could leave the rope and pick here… mark our spot? It'd be easier to look for the morels in the morning anyways… I don't want to wait too much longer for you… could you please at least let me have a flash—?"

The sound of stone cracking on stone interrupted Reinhardt. Then for a moment all was quiet. Slowly the sounds of animal life began to creep under the leaves at his feet and creak on the limbs above his head.

"Jonah! Jonah, stop it!" His voice sounded muffled by the woods. He ran forward a step into the thicket to follow Jonah's path, but past the first thicket, he could not see in the dark where his older brother had gone. "JO-NAH!!" His final scream cracked as tears came on. He ran for home.

11

THE SUN had sunk below the horizon, yet the lingering greyness stifled the light of stars in the west. Reinhardt ran across the farmyard and into the house.

"What's wrong, Reinhardt?" Eleanor asked.

"Jonah left me in the woods."

"He did what?"

"He was mad at me and went off; before I knew it, he was out of sight and hiding from me. I waited, but the noises started to freak me out, and he wouldn't stop hiding! And it was getting dark, so I ran home."

"All this just happened?"

He nodded. His face was still smudged and damp with tears. Eleanor used a kitchen towel in an attempt to wipe his face, but he squirmed. "Go wash up and have some food." From the counter she put together a plate. Reinhardt washed his hands and face then returned to the table. Eleanor turned the porch light on and stared out the window. She looked to Reinhardt, she looked back out the window.

"I'm not hungry, Mom."

"I'm going out on the porch," she said.

"I'll come with you," he said, jumping up from his seat. Together they stood out on the porch. The house lights shone on the front lawn; Grandma's summer kitchen windows were all alight too. Eleanor walked across the lawn to Grandma's and knocked on her door.

"What is it, Eleanor, you look tense?" Grandma asked. Though the night was considerably warm for early spring, she was wrapped up in a quilt and was already wearing an old-fashioned night cap.

"Jonah is still out, and I'm becoming a bit worried. I'm going to walk down the lane to the woods, only I'm waiting for a call from Noah. Would you mind much?"

"Oh, not at all, how long has Jonah been out?" The ladies looked across the lawn to Reinhardt; he was leaning over the porch rail. "How long have you guys been out?" Eleanor yelled across the lawn.

"After stacking logs, we went out to the woods."

"Hours."

Grandma popped on her work boots, swapped her night cap for a wool felt hat, and grabbed a bag from a hook by the door. They crossed the lawn.

Eleanor asked, "Reinhardt, will you get a flashlight?"

"We took all the flashlights," he said. "They're in the backpack Jonah took."

"You didn't tell me that; what else did you haul out there? Wait, Mother, do you have any flashlights?"

"I have just the thing," Grandma said. She walked back across the lawn, hung the bag up, popped off her boots, and disappeared inside.

"What else did you take to the woods?" Eleanor repeated.

"Well, that's why I went at all. See, Jonah needed help carrying supplies. At first, he—well, I just thought I better help him, and we were on the hunt for morels, but then he wanted to stay out so long, and I was tired of carrying the pack, the pack that had the flashlights and some water and stuff like that. And the sun was setting, so that's when he got angry with me..."

Grandma returned. "This will have to do, my dears," she said, holding up a lantern. "It's actually quite nice, see?" She turned it on and twisted a knob that expanded and contracted the shutter. "Noah just gave it to me. It's a neat old thing, strong light."

***

Mother and son walked the lane. Clouds scattered the sky, but through them a waning gibbous helped illuminate the path. They neared the edge of the woods; the lantern light reflected off the side of the metal Quonset and proved of little use for seeing into the woods.

"Jonah!" Eleanor called out several times. "I wonder if he came up already. She looked on both ends of the Quonset. All the lights were off inside, the windows on the west end were dark. They stood still, listening, waiting. She asked, "Should we try walking in the woods?"

"The woods sound so creepy during the night," Reinhardt said. "Maybe Jonah came up from the other end?"

"Did you come up from this side?"

"I came back this way." Reinhardt nodded.

"Let's go back home," Eleanor said.

Returning home, they saw Grandma sitting in the rocking chair knitting.

"Did Noah ring?" Eleanor asked.

Grandma's fingers continued on; her gaze glazed over in her work. She gave a gentle shake of her head that matched the rhythm of her rocking. "All's quiet here."

"No sign of Jonah?"

"All's quiet as a church mouse."

"I'm starting to get worried," Eleanor said. "If Noah hasn't called by now, that means he's probably headed home and has been driving since dinner. Son, you really ought to eat something." The plate of food sat cold on the table. Reinhardt took his seat and picked at the food. Eleanor continued, "Maybe I should call Pastor John."

"I'm just not hungry, Mom."

"That's fine, dear." She joined him, her elbows on the table, hands folded with her forehead resting against them.

"Are you okay, Mom?"

"I'm just thinking, praying. Your brother has got me worried, and if I don't hear from him or your father pretty soon, I'm going to be a basket-case."

"Call Pastor John then," Grandma said. "Noah may not be home for another hour or two. Jonah's probably trying to harass his brother by staying out, unknowingly to the detriment of his mother and soon everyone else…" she trailed off into an undecipherable mumble and began knitting with renewed vigor.

"I'm afraid I'll block the line," Eleanor responded more to herself than to Grandma.

They all sat in silence listening to the *nix-nix* of the knitting needles and the gentle sway and creak of the rocking chair.

After a few minutes, Eleanor said, "I'm sorry, Mother. You don't have to stay, I forgot…" Just then the phone rang and she sprang to it. "Hello?"

"Hello, Ella," came the voice of Noah on the other end of the line.

"Oh, thank goodness it's you," she exhaled. "Please tell me you're not staying the night."

"Sorry, I wasn't even going to call, I'm nearly home, I left late, and now I had to stop for gas. I'm at Certified; they let me use the phone. Do you need me to pick up a gallon of milk?"

"Can you please just hurry home?"

"What's wrong?"

"Everyone's fine, I think, just Jonah hasn't come in yet, and it's getting pretty late."

"He didn't go out with that girl?"

"No, no, heavens no, Reinhardt and him were in the woods. Reinhardt came up a while ago, but not Jonah."

"Alright, well I'm just up at Certified. I'll be right home."

"Okay, thanks," Eleanor said.

"I'll grab some milk and fresh batteries too. Love you."

"Love you too. Oh, wait—" she heard the phone line terminate, "…there aren't any flashlights." Standing by the wall phone, she palmed her face. She took a deep breath, then grabbed the phone book from the shelf and searched the "C's."

"Mom, will you come sit with me?" Reinhardt was at the couch now.

"Of course, one moment." She found the Certified Gas and Market phone number and called back, but the line was busy. She gave up and joined her son on the couch. The *nix-nix* of the knitting and the rocking of the chair continued. Eventually, they heard the rev of the truck coming up the lane.

Noah parked the Chevy in the barnyard. From the passenger side, he brought out two jugs of milk. He handed them to his son. "Go run these inside please. And bring out some more flashlights."

"Jonah and Reinhardt took all the flashlights to the woods," Eleanor said. "But we have this." She held up the lantern Grandma had given her.

"Oh, right, that thing." Noah frowned. He took the lantern from his wife and placed it out of sight on the floorboards of the truck cab.

"Did you intend to stay in the woods all night?" Noah asked Reinhardt.

Reinhardt shook his head.

"Okay, thankfully I've got one in here." Noah brought out a bulky flashlight from the truck glovebox and put some fresh batteries in.

"Who's that coming up the lane?" Eleanor asked.

"Pastor John," Noah said. Eleanor gave him a confused look. He added, "I called him up at Certified."

"I was just considering doing the same thing, calling him— especially when I didn't know if you were coming home."

"Well, sounds like we're on the same page." He winked. Seeing Eleanor was not much at ease, he gave her a hug and kiss. "Don't be worried, Ella. John and I will walk the woods. I'm sure he's fine."

Pastor John parked his vehicle. "Good evening, Brandtmeyers."

From the porch the voice of Reinhardt yelled, "Who's that?"

"Pastor John," his mom said.

Reinhardt came over to them and asked, "The two of you are going out there?"

"Not wise to walk in the woods alone at night," Pastor John said.

"Wild animals?" Reinhardt asked with wide eyes, but a yawn overtook him. The day had left him tired and disheveled.

"Lord willing, your expression will be the wildest thing we see all night. We're more likely to be sprayed by skunks than come across any animal that's really dangerous," said Pastor John.

Noah said, "There's more of a chance to trip and fall and break your leg in the dark, that's all. Head back inside now, stay with your mother, and keep her company, please."

"Grandma's inside. I want to come along."

"Please stay inside. There's one lantern for Pastor John and this flashlight for me." He held up his flashlight. "I don't want you tripping in the dark and getting hurt." He looked to Eleanor and added, "And your mother would appreciate the extra company."

Eleanor put her arm around Reinhardt. "Come on, son. Let's keep watch on the porch for your brother. It's like you said earlier, maybe he already came up, or soon will." She directed her attention to her husband. "Please be careful, dear."

"He'll track Jonah down, and I'll make sure Noah doesn't lose his track." Pastor John offered with a smile. Noah handed him the lantern.

"Here John, this one for walking," he held up his flashlight, "and this one for searching. Let's go."

Noah and Pastor John headed up the lane with the flashlight swaying to the north across the creek, then to the south over the fields. All was quiet.

"How was the interview?" John asked.

"Thanks again for the recommendation."

"It's the least I can do," John said.

"They definitely liked me. Your brother coordinated a meeting with his superior today. I was there the whole day. When it came to brass tacks, I just don't think I have the experience they need for the position."

"Is it a closed deal? Maybe I could call him up. You may have been too modest with your abilities."

"Let me think it over. Yesterday I put the money from the Wood-Mizer sale into the farm loan, but that only buys us time. I'm afraid we're going to continue to bleed cash while we pray for a miracle. The idea of moving my family to Indiana to take advantage of a great job is daunting; I haven't broken it to my sons as a possibility. And it's like you said, our community is here, and accepting the job would change all that."

"And where does Eleanor stand?"

"She understands the position we're in. I didn't even have the chance this evening to tell her how things went."

"How long since Jonah's been out?"

"Just this evening by the sound of things. I had called you up from the gas station and only arrived minutes before you." Noah shook his head and said with a grim chuckle, "Reminds me when you've spoken of coming home from a long day— looking forward to food on the table, all the family well, but when you walk in the door, all is chaos. Only I didn't even make it through the front door."

Pastor John smiled.

The soft light from the waning gibbous caused the metal of the Quonset to shimmer in the night like a woodland mausoleum. Noah pushed open the shop office door and flipped on the light switch exposing the desk wreckage spewed across the floor.

"Interesting," Noah said. He crouched down next to the desk and rummaged through the contents. He looked up to the shelf, went to it, straightened up the books and took an inventory. "All accounted for."

"What's that?"

"My Dad's old journals; my son likes to read them. They're all here."

"What happened to the desk?"

"I'm sure Jonah will be able to enlighten us." Noah scratched his chin. From the debris, he grabbed a pen and paper and scrawled a note.

"Maybe I was too hard on Jonah yesterday." Noah told John the story of the escaped Berkshires and his sons running off with Leslie. "And," he added, "I had just come from the bank. I hand delivered to Mr. Schreiber my check. Then confirmed his daughter and Jonah's new acquaintance are one in the same! So, you can imagine the awkwardness of that conversation, only an hour later, when I rang him up to explain what his daughter had been up to. He was quite embarrassed and apologized." Noah paused a moment in thought.

"And," Pastor John asked.

"Perhaps he planned to meet with that girl again. Well, one thing at a time, let's search the woods, but if our search is unsuccessful, I'll call Mr. Schreiber and see if he knows anything. When I spoke with him it was cordial. I was thankful for that; you know how awkward those conversations can be."

"I'm well acquainted."

"As I was saying, yesterday I ended up taking a pretty hard line with Jonah. He had given me attitude in the morning, and then followed it up in the afternoon. He's reached this age where big decisions carry big consequences. I was upset with him for foolishly getting into a car with a girl, unknown to us mind you, who got her license the day of, leaves with her, not telling anyone... so irresponsible—and to take his little brother with him, also setting a terrible example. I talked to him, and none of this even crossed his mind when I asked him about it: just a pretty girl, in a nice car, getting ice cream. Oh, and he stole money from our little cash reserve."

"That sounds dishonoring enough," Pastor John said.

"Enough to give him the belt?"

"Ah," Pastor John curled his lips inward and nodded in thought. "'He who spares the rod...' however, Jonah's becoming a young man, and certain disciplines can backfire. Tough age for sure."

"I'm concerned that's just it, a turn towards more recklessness, or rebellion, or both."

"Let us pray this immediate circumstance is unrelated, but only a brief incident of a boy seeking a late-night adventure and has merely lost his way returning home."

"Amen to that." They exited the shop office; Noah left the lights on allowing a pleasant glow to shine out the windows. He tacked the note he had written to the door: "Your mother and I are looking for you, Jonah. You have all of us concerned. Please come home. Love, Dad."

The two men followed the west border, and finding the first gate of the fence line ajar, they followed the pig trail through the woods, and spent over an hour calling and searching for Jonah.

***

"Find anything?" Eleanor stood in the doorway.

"No sign of him in the woods," Noah said, "but honestly, it's just too dark to make a thorough search. While out though, it crossed my mind perhaps he intended to sneak off? It sounds ridiculous, but as a precaution I thought we might as well call up Leslie's parents."

"You don't think? But, if you didn't find him…" she trailed off and wringed her hands.

"Don't despair," Pastor John said as he set the lantern on the porch, "there are still many possibilities."

"Of course, of course," Eleanor tried convincing herself. "Could I get you something to drink, Pastor John?"

Inside Noah dialed the Schreiber's.

"Hello, Mr. Schreiber. Sorry to bother you so late at night, it's just," Noah stammered, "in light of recent events, and this is rather embarrassing, but it would seem Jonah has disappeared and I just thought, not that I'm making any accusations, but thought maybe he tried sneaking out to meet with your daughter?" On the other end Mr. Schreiber said something. Noah responded, "Ah, okay. Well thank you, if you see him, please call... Thank you, we appreciate that... I don't think that's necessary... Absolutely... Thanks, Mr. Schreiber, good-bye." Noah hung the telephone back on its hook. He turned to Eleanor, "Leslie's at home grounded, on account of yesterday I presume—I didn't ask. Mr. Schreiber offered to help look. I don't think Jonah has met him though; either way, he said he'd call in the morning just to check in."

"Oh, that's nice of him."

Noah nodded; he stood in the hallway by the phone. Pastor John was drinking a glass of water and standing in the front entryway. "I can make a trip around the block in my car?" He said.

"I'll come along," Noah said. "Are you okay with me leaving, Eleanor?"

She nodded. "I'll stay with Reinhardt. He fell asleep on the couch."

The two men drove around the block. After driving down Bay Road, Noah said, "Let's turn it around here, John. The next intersection is Center Road in half a mile, and we haven't seen a thing."

"You want to head back the way we came?"

Noah nodded.

Pastor John turned around at the intersection of Bay Road and Burr Oak. They drove slowly and in silence.

As they pulled back into the lane for home, Noah said, "Jonah took all the flashlights in the house. Why would he have done that?"

John frowned and shook his head. "He planned to be out late."

Noah sighed heavily. "Maybe he planned to run off. He's upset enough, whether justified or not. A fourteen-year-old probably feels being 'upset' is enough justification to run off."

"Maybe he planned to camp in the woods?"

"Maybe."

Back in the house, Noah shared the uneventful trip with Eleanor. Reinhardt woke to the sounds of their conversation. He could hear the concern and growing worry in his mother's voice as she said, "Jonah did find out you were interviewing for the job in Indiana. Maybe he did plan to run away." Reinhardt mustered his strength and came to the front door where the adults assembled.

"Mom, Dad."

"Reinhardt."

"Jonah was really looking for morels; I don't think he intended to actually leave the woods. He wanted to go deeper into the woods; that's what made me turn back."

"You don't think he planned to run away?" Noah asked.

"If so, there were no feelings I had—feelings that he would run off." Reinhardt was searching for words, his parents, and Pastor John too, could read it all over his tired face. "See, Jonah knew a spot, he had a map from one of Granddad's journals."

Noah cocked his head. "A map? Which year?"

"I didn't see. He didn't show me the journal."

"I know of no maps in his journals, all the journals were on the shelf, I just checked earlier," Noah said. "Are you sure it was one of Granddad's journals, or—"

"It was most definitely one; I could see that as plain as day, and Jonah said it was one of his journals. That reminds me, the last thing Jonah yelled, or said was 'Don't tell Dad,' but I don't even know why he said that. I think it's because he was angry I wanted to go home, and that's just one of his things he yells when he's mad at me, 'Don't tell Dad!'" he shrugged. "I was just thinking about what you said yesterday."

"Thanks, son," he patted Reinhardt's shoulder, "I appreciate that. It's really late. I want you to try to get some sleep." Noah eyed Reinhardt as he left the room.

"What are you thinking?" Eleanor asked.

Noah was biting his upper lip in thought. "The desk in the Quonset was tipped over, broke some of the paneling, really quite an extravagant mess for one desk to make, a desk I suppose has been stuffed with clutter for several years." He paused in thought. "All the journals were on the shelf." Noah looked to his wife and continued his trail of reasoning, "It's possible Dad had another journal, and Jonah found it."

"And with it he found a clue?" she asked.

"Good Lord, if that's true! Jonah isn't looking for morels. He's looking for Dad."

12

BEFORE the light of day, Noah made another trip around the block. Grey skies and roadkill left him looking dismal as he returned to the farm. Eleanor was sitting on the porch swing. He made to sit by her, but suddenly she held up the lantern.

"Noah, your mother gave me this lantern last night." Eleanor fiddled with the knob. "It's a neat little lantern. Where did we get it?"

Noah stepped back and grimaced as if the lantern stunk. "This just keeps coming back to haunt me." He steeled up his frame and continued, "It was a harebrained idea, but I had every intention of grave digging."

Eleanor's eyes widened. She looked horrified.

"I didn't go through with it," Noah explained, "but that day in Al's store I bought the lantern for that purpose. It was stupid; I was feeling desperate."

Eleanor set the lantern down as if it was a maggot-riddled loaf of bread. An awkward silence followed, then she asked, "Why didn't you go through with it?"

"Grave digging?" Noah asked. "It was the scripture reading on Good Friday." He stepped inside to grab his muck boots.

Returning to the porch, he called for Captain. Captain didn't come.

"That dog is useless." He gave a slim smile. Eleanor did not give a response. Noah continued, "I thought maybe I'd find something of value in those graves. When Pastor John read about the graves being opened it reminded me that those graves hold the remains of real people, people no different than us."

Eleanor nodded slightly and wiped tears from her cheeks. Noah handed her his pocket handkerchief. "I'm just terrified about Jonah," she said in a strained voice, "what if he disappears forever too?" She began to sob.

Noah sat next to her and squeezed her hand. He was fighting back tears. For several minutes the two sat there on the porch swing. Once the wave of hopelessness passed, Noah said, "Look, I wanted to head down to the woods, just to check the Quonset. Would you like to join me?"

She shook her head. "I'll stay here. I want someone to be around if he suddenly returns home."

Noah nodded in agreement.

A red dawn crept over the branches of the woods. Noah trekked again along the potholed path to the Quonset and checked inside. The room was empty. He flipped the light switch off. Then he walked along the edge of the woods. The tall spring grass polished the surface of his black muck boots, but there was little dew on the grass. "'When grass is dry at morning light, look for rain before the night.'" he muttered to himself, "but not today, Lord, not yet."

Birds chirped with the dawning sun. He called Jonah's name several times with no response. When he returned home, Pastor John was already there drinking coffee on the porch.

"News?" the pastor asked.

"Nothing. You?"

"Just strengthened with a night of prayer and researching maps of the area."

"Thanks for both." Noah leaned on the porch rail for a moment then said, "It's still quite possible Jonah meant to camp out. When Reinhardt wakes up, I'll have him lead us to where they were. In the meantime…" Noah paused, then stepped inside and called the sheriff's office.

Pastor John followed him in. "Thanks for the coffee, Eleanor."

"You're welcome," she said. After Noah hung up the phone, Eleanor handed him a cup. "Have some coffee, dear. What did they say?"

"Thanks," Noah said. "They filed a report and said they'd send Deputy Ransburg to all the neighboring farms to inquire if they had seen or housed a Jonah Brandtmeyer for the night. They'll call right away if they find him or 'news of his whereabouts.'"

Noah blew on the black coffee, shuffled restlessly around the kitchen, tilted his head listening, and looked at the ceiling. "I'm tempted to wake Reinhardt now."

Eleanor looked at the ceiling too. "Maybe I should go up and wake him?"

They shuffled back out to the porch. It was morning; the roosters were trumpeting. The red dawn illuminated the clouds in a colorful display of red and pink hues. Streaks of yellow sunlight came bursting across the landscape casting shadows behind them into a distant west.

"I'm not one for omens," Noah muttered, "curse them, but the saying goes, 'Red sky in morning—"

"I'm waking Reinhardt up," Eleanor interrupted. She went back inside. From the porch, the men heard the creaking upstairs, and before a rooster let out another morning trumpet, Reinhardt was on the porch, dressed, and wide awake.

"Are we headed out?" he asked. "I'm ready, let's go!"

***

He first led them to the cliff-like bank in the woods. "This is where Jonah showed me the map. We wanted to get up there." He pointed out the top of a fallen tree above the bank and brambles.

Pastor John was taking notes in his little notepad. "What was Jonah's purpose?" he asked.

"He said Granddad discovered a trove of morels up there."

They followed the path from yesterday, which brought them out on the east side of the woods. As they emerged, the sun was blotted out by grey clouds.

"The clouds are gathering," Noah remarked, "and it smells like rain."

"Is that Bay Road across this field?" Pastor John asked, pointing across a fresh sown field.

"Yes," said Noah, "that's the road that makes up the east side of our block."

"Right, just wanted to confirm," and he made some more lines and marks in his notepad.

Reinhardt said, "It's just right over here now." He took them to where he had left the rope and pick-adze on the ground. "Here's where Jonah went back into the woods. I didn't because it was too dark."

Noah investigated the thickets that barred the wood line. A few small twigs were snapped suggesting his son may have pushed through. He called out Jonah's name; all three listened quietly. No response came.

"I don't know, Dad, maybe he isn't just camping. Maybe..." Reinhardt's words caught in his throat and he kicked his boot against the pile of rope. He started to tear up.

Noah knelt down and put a hand on Reinhardt's shoulder. "We'll find him, son."

"Maybe he wasn't looking for morels after all," the boy cried, "maybe he is running away! Why else did he take all this stuff?"

Noah looked to Pastor John.

Pastor John said, "Exactly, Reinhardt, why did he take all this stuff if he was intending to run off? Why the rope and pick? Why would he have even brought you out here in the first place? It doesn't make sense. Stay calm now; let's enter the woods here."

Noah nodded. "Pastor John is right, Reinhardt. Come on, I can see signs that we are on the right track; you've led us successfully this far. Let me take the lead now." Noah stood up tall.

Reinhardt rubbed the tears out of his eyes and mustered his confidence. "Okay."

The going was filled with snags. Untouched by humans and foraging Berkshires, the woods had become overgrown. Vines braided themselves with branches above. Widow-makers hung overhead.

"This is a rather unpleasant section of the woods," Pastor John stated. He had retired his notepad and pen to a pocket. "What possessed Jonah to go this way?"

"Granddad found morels here," Reinhardt said.

"Is that poison ivy?" Pastor John pointed to a tree trunk completely covered in dense vines yet without foliage.

Noah looked at it from a safe distance. "Too early for me to tell, but probably, don't touch." He continued to lead the way, now and again stopping to discern the path. They had only gone several yards into the area, and it had proven to be as fortified as it looked from the outside. "I'm confident someone went through here, and not a deer or some such animal, these broken thorns don't have fur stuck on them. He held up a strand, "It's not much, but this is a piece of cotton thread." His face was tense with anticipation and hope. "Let's keep going. It wasn't much of a walk around the outskirts; this whole area can't be much more than a dozen square yards. I can see the spot of the fallen tree. It looks like Jonah made for that direction."

They continued and the brambles began to lighten. Suddenly they came upon a clearing. Four-petaled purple beauties called "Dame's Rocket" coated the ground. The fallen oak laid across the midst, its trunk extending west towards the natural hedge and cliff. Its old lifeless branches, tangled in the brush, protruded high into the air above. Near them was the great root bulb, massive in size, that had ripped the earth open in its destruction. The roots of the oak were a network of grubby tubular growth packed with clods of dirt and large stones—stones that had been caught up in the growth, captured by decades of the slowly growing roots, like fingers closing in around a ball. The whole mass was like a scab torn half way off the flesh of the earth, leaving a sizeable crater in the ground. In the earthen bowl, more large stones were rent by roots.

Noah looked at all this, then to the greying sky. "Usually spots like this, where a tree has fallen, fills with rain water," he explained. "Like a little pool. This one is bone dry."

At the same time, Pastor John stooped down by a neighboring slippery elm; around the trunk's base a much-weathered rope, decaying and frayed, was tied.

Noah stepped down into the crater for a closer look. One of the stones looked like it had endured a fresh scrape, like it had moved across another stone. "'The rocks were rent...'" Noah murmured. "'The rocks were rent; and...'"

"Noah, look at this—" John began, but his words were cut off by a loud scrape and crack of stone on stone. From the corner of his eye, he caught the sight of Noah vanishing into the earth. Like a natural trapdoor a slab of stone snapped back into place. Reinhardt screamed in terror.

"Noah!" John shouted. Stones and dirt covered the spot where Noah had stood. "Noah! Can you hear me?" He listened. Reinhardt was shaking and crying at his side. "Reinhardt," Pastor John knelt down and put his hands on the boy's shoulders in an attempt to steady him. "Reinhardt, take a deep breath. Calm down, son. Did you see what happened?"

"Dad just," Reinhardt made a flailing motion with his hands. "I don't know! He just disappeared into the ground!" Tears were choking his speech.

Looking to the crater, then to heaven, then to the path from which they emerged, John said, "Bay Road, Reinhardt, that's the road across that field. What's the intersection just to the north?"

Tears soaked Reinhardt's cheeks. "I... I don't know," he stammered.

"Wiefenbach." Pastor John procured his notepad and wrote the name down, "and Bay Road." Say it back to me.

"Wiefenbach and Bay."

"Here." John handed him the little piece of paper. "You can run fast, you know the way home, run home, tell your mother to call the fire department, tell them to meet Pastor John at this intersection," he pointed to the paper in Reinhardt's hand, "and tell them there's been a cave in, and we'll need to do some digging." He nudged the boy towards the path they had come in by. "That's the way out, okay, Reinhardt? Now run!"

After he sent Reinhardt on his way, he went back to the crater. He confirmed his suspicion: the rope from the slippery elm ended at the craters edge, old and mangled, with a few threads pinched under a stone.

"Noah!" He called in a loud voice, he listened again. On hands and knees, he reached down into the crater; he saw marks made from stone sliding against stone, but from his secure position, the stones were out of reach.

He ran back to the border of the woods for the rope and pick-adze. Then he tied the fresh rope around the same tree as the old one, and with a firm grasp on the rope in his left hand and the pick-adze in his right, he tested the stones with some prying. A few drops of rain began falling and Pastor John slipped a little. He came up out of the crater shaking his head and talking to himself.

"What are you trying to do, John? What's the goal here?" With a furrowed brow and closed eyes, he said, "'Can a man hide himself in secret places? Do I not fill heaven and earth?' John, you are of absolutely no use if you fall down there too." He set the pick-adze and rope down. The rainfall began in earnest and soaked his head and shoulders.

"Noah!" John shouted again over the sound of the rain, "If you can hear me, I'm going to get the fire department. I'll be back with help. Hang on!"

***

Noah tried to stand but wavered and remained seated. It had been a rough trip; he had gone head over heels and at least a dozen feet down, but had landed feet first when he came to a complete stop. Throbbing began in his ankle. He felt for blood and in the dark could not feel any, though his ankle was swelling. "Sprained? Broken?" He spit dirt out of his mouth and felt his chest. "No broken ribs."

Out of utter darkness, a small point of light clicked into being. He blinked and attempted to rub the stars from his eyes, but the pale light remained and wobbled closer. There was a whimpering sound that accompanied it. The light suddenly shone directly at him, making him hold up his hand to block the beam from his eyes.

"Dad?" The voice was shaky, "Dad, you found us!" The form of a bedraggled boy materialized as Noah's vision adjusted. "Oh, Dad," he wailed and threw himself on his father.

"Jonah!" Noah squeezed him tight. "You're here; where is here? Where in the world are we?"

"We fell into a cavern," Jonah said and released his grip on his dad to shine a light up on the ceiling. "I think we fell in from over there." He used the flashlight to point. "I tried climbing back up that way, but it's impossibly steep... there was an old rope," Jonah croaked, and began a fresh wave of uncontrollable sobs.

"It's okay, son, it's okay." Noah put his arms around Jonah. "Reinhardt and Pastor John are above us. They probably think I'm crushed. They'll get us out."

This intensified Jonah's cries even more; he was nearly raving. "Crushed! Crushed! The rope, it was rotten, rotten away."

"Rotten rope? We saw the rope you brought. What rope?"

"Not so loud," Jonah whispered, "must not yell for help, or more will come down and crush us too."

"Jonah, calm down, I'm here now. You are going to be okay."

"Dad, we aren't the only ones down here." Jonah's face, through the dirt and tears, was a sickly green. He handed his dad a flashlight. "There." Noah followed the extended arm of his son with the flashlight.

"Ah!" Noah gasped. The weak light exposed, crushed under a boulder, a skeleton.

Noah drew near, palms clammy, forehead in a sweat. From the wrist bone glinted the tarnished Bulova watch. Noah touched the artifact. His body shook and seasoned tears flooded down his face. The cavern ceiling was made of boulders and dirt like the masonry work of an ancient giant. A boulder from above had dislodged and crushed the body of the old Brandtmeyer.

Noah noticed the floor was wet. "Is the entire crypt mourning with us?" he said, half delirious. A shine of the light revealed water trickling down from above. It dripped like tears from juts of rock all around. After gathering himself, he said, "I think it's begun to rain."

Rainwater began to pool on the cavern floor. Noah attempted to push the boulder off the remains of his father. Jonah joined the effort. Together they struggled to shift the boulder. The water level continued to rise, drowning the bones that were pinned underneath.

Suddenly, their tomb shone with the dull grey of a rain filled sky. The whole place glistened in the wash of water and light. Above, an opening had been wrested. Frightened voices shouted from on high—the cries of Eleanor and Reinhardt, even the barking of Captain. The voice of Pastor John shouted, "Noah! Noah, are you alive? We can't see anything down there!"

A member of the volunteer fire department descended on a fresh rope. The man wore a helmet with a search-lamp. Noah and Jonah were stunned by the excessive amount of light. They watched the spelunker as he cautiously worked his way down. Once he reached the water, he stopped and looked around.

"We're here." Noah called, still blinking and squinting. "We're here. We're well." The man spotted Noah and his son, both of them held their hands up to block the light. "We are okay!" Noah shouted up into the light.

"They're okay!" the firefighter agreed. "And there are two of them!"

Shouts of excitement and great sighs of relief could be heard from above. Pastor John shouted, "Did you hear!? There are two of them!"

13

Spring was in full bloom. Johnny Jump-ups were jumping up between the cracks in the sidewalks. Tulips, like dozens of colorful cups, lined the walkways in the small town. Magnolia petals, thick and white, blew off the tree's branches in the corner of the church cemetery. The petals tumbled among the stone markers and became trampled under the black shoes of those gathered. Pastor John read from the Psalms:

> "'In thee, O Jehovah, do I take refuge;
> Let me never be put to shame:
> Deliver me in thy righteousness.
> Bow down thine ear unto me;
> Deliver me speedily:
> Be thou to me a strong rock,
> A house of defence to save me.'"

Grandma cried into a handkerchief, and Eleanor had her arms around her. Noah stood beside them, propped up by crutches, recovering from a sprained ankle. Jonah and Reinhardt watched as those gathered dropped their flowers into the grave.

"'For thou art my rock and my fortress;
Therefore for thy name's sake lead me and guide me.
Pluck me out of the net that they have laid privily for me;
For thou art my stronghold.
Into thy hand I commend my spirit:
Thou hast redeemed me, O Jehovah, thou God of truth.'"

The body was laid to rest. The final flower dropped. The community meandered into the shadow cast by the church steeple and waited for their chance to pay their respects to the Brandtmeyers. Jonah lingered by his grandfather's open grave. He knelt down and peered into the pit. White roses covered the top of the casket.

Jonah whispered:

"'I went down to the bottoms of the mountains;
The earth with its bars *closed* upon me for ever:
Yet hast thou bought up my life from the pit,
O Jehovah my God.
When my soul fainted within me,
I remembered Jehovah;
And my prayer came in unto thee,'
I memorized that for you, Granddad."

A girl's soft voice came from behind Jonah. "Sounds genuine. Did you come up with that?"

Jonah turned and stood up. "Leslie, I didn't expect you here," he stammered. "Grounded and all."

"My dad brought me," she said. A magnolia blossom was fixed in her hair. "Sorry for your loss, Jonah. And I really mean it, not like when some people just say it." She offered a sympathetic smile.

"I'm sorry about last week, with the police." Jonah frowned at the ground.

Leslie nodded.

"What happened with the cop?" He continued.

"I got a ticket."

"I'm sorry, Leslie. It's my fault."

"Oh, and I have to do community service, specifically trash pick-up. But that's my parents' doing."

"Let me know the dates; I'll join you," Jonah offered.

"Thanks, Jonah." She brightened up a bit. "I was pretty upset with you…"

"Really?" Jonah cringed.

"…And with the situation. I blamed you, I blamed myself, but when I heard you went missing… it helped me to stop thinking only about myself." They both were quiet for a moment. Then she continued, "You must have been so terrified. Trapped underground, completely in the dark… then with," she indicated the grave, "well, you know what I mean." She shuddered then asked, "What was it like?"

"You know the story of Jonah and the whale?"

Leslie smirked, "Like the nursery rhyme Sunday school stuff?"

"Well, no, not exactly… Jonah gets swallowed up, and he's pretty much at death's door, but on the third day the whale vomits him up. I didn't really know the story either, but while I was down there," Jonah looked to the open pit his grandfather now rested in, "it was for my namesake I told myself to hold on to hope… for at least three days. It was the fear of the days following that terrified me."

"Sounds terrifying from day one," Leslie said.

Jonah sank his head between his shoulders and tried to hide a tear by brushing it aside. Leslie put her arm around him.

136

"Let's sit on that bench under the tree with these pretty white flowers," she said, touching the blossom in her hair.

"It's a Magnolia."

"I like a guy who knows his flowers." Leslie smiled.

"You would have liked my granddad then."

"I think I like you."

And Jonah rubbed his ear.

One after another offered their condolences and left the church cemetery. Grandma sat by her late husband's gravestone. Jonah remained under the Magnolia with Leslie. Reinhardt walked along the cemetery's border. The parents were speaking with Pastor John, and patiently waiting until the pastor took his leave, one other man remained: Leslie's father, Don Schreiber. When his opportunity came, he approached the Brandtmeyers. His warm countenance in the sunshine made him momentarily unrecognizable.

Noah raised his eyebrows in surprise. "Oh, hello, Mr. Schreiber."

He smiled shyly, stammered, and then cleared his throat. "Sorry for your loss, Mr. and Mrs. Brandtmeyer. Sincerely."

"Thank you," Eleanor said.

"Thank you for offering your respect," Noah said.

"I know now isn't the place, but I'm nearly bursting at the seams to go over all the good news. Stop by my office sometime this week? Whenever you're ready. Not only is your farm secured through your father's credit life insurance, but it appears all the payments you have been making on it for the last two years will be returned to you as well—with interest." Mr. Schreiber beamed.

"Wow, Mr. Schreiber, that's incredible news." Noah and Eleanor were elated.

"Come by this week, and we'll get all the paperwork set in stone."

"Thank you, Mr. Schreiber."

"I come from a big city; the bank transferred me here," Mr. Schreiber spread his arms out, "to play hardball with these small towns, and from a bank's perspective, with the little man with his little loans." He gave out a grim chuckle. "These little loans that crush the little man. The point is, it's easy to remain distant in a city and treat a man as an asset or liability, but these small town connections grow on you—makes it hard to see the man as a number. No hard feelings?"

Noah smiled. "None at all, Mr. Schreiber."

"Thanks." He extended his hand. "You can call me Don."

Noah balanced on one crutch and shook Don's hand. Noah nodded over to where his son was sitting under the tree. "Speaking of small town connections, have you met my son, Jonah?"

"Oh, that reminds me of another matter." Don waved for his daughter. "Leslie, come here please." She and Jonah came. "These are Jonah's parents. I believe you had something to say to them?"

She flushed but said, "Sorry for taking your sons out without permission."

Eleanor and Noah forgave her.

Jonah said, "I told her to go fast, I don't think she would have run the light if it weren't for me... Oh, and we wouldn't have lost our root beer floats. Sorry, Mom and Dad. Sorry, Mr. Schreiber. I'd like to help Leslie with trash pick-up for what it's worth."

"I forgive you, Jonah." Don said. "And I'm sure Leslie would be grateful for the company."

Eleanor suggested, "Let's schedule a time to have your family over for dinner."

"We'll treat you to our Brandtmeyer Berkshire bacon," Noah added.

"That's most generous of you, thank you," Don said.

Leslie, however, put two and two together and her face quivered. "Wait, those piglets are for eating?"

***

Reinhardt sat on the bench in the mudroom putting on his shoes. Jonah stood by him picking at the leather lacing of a baseball mitt. "Hey Reinhardt, I know I can be a bit of a jerk and treat you like crap…" Jonah frowned, "but, I'm working on it, alright?"

"Okay, Jonah. I know. You…" Reinhardt trailed off.

"'You' what?"

"You could start by not calling me Reiner."

Jonah pondered this, and then asked, "What about 'Reinster'?"

"That's really not any shorter than Reinhardt."

"Doesn't sound like Whiner," Jonah said, "Reinster—has a nice ring to it, don't you think?"

"Sure, you can try it out."

"Okay, come on, let's go play some catch." The boys went out to the front yard. Under the two massive catalpas, the boys began their game. Grandma and Eleanor were swinging on the porch watching them. Assisted with a cane, Noah came up from the lane carrying the mail. Captain emerged from the windbreak to join him.

"Fetch, Cap'n!" Jonah yelled when he saw Captain come to the yard. He chucked the baseball over the dog's head. Captain went and fetched it.

"He's coming around," Jonah said.

"That he is," Noah agreed and walked over to where the ladies sat. "Newspaper arrived. Has Dad's obituary. It's really nice."

"We'll have to frame it," Grandma said.

"We can hang it up in Granddad's old shop," Jonah suggested.

"I was thinking in the house, or at your grandmother's," Eleanor said.

"We can drive into town later and pick up a few more copies," Noah said. "One for everyone." Then he laughed and shook his head.

"That's a fine idea, what's wrong?" Eleanor asked.

"Of course, we'll have multiple copies so I'll never forget the other matter. Read the front page headline." He handed her the paper.

She read it out loud, "Local Businessman Albrecht "Al" Katterheinrich Caught in Statewide Illegal Arms Dealing Operation." She looked wide-eyed at her husband. "That's the pawn shop guy?"

"'Clean as the driven snow,'" Noah quoted, leaning on his cane and grinning. "That's what Emerson said."

"Hmm." Eleanor seemed unimpressed. "I'd say you narrowly escaped involvement 'by the skin of your teeth.'"

Noah nodded in agreement. "That too, that too."

"What's all this about?" Grandma asked.

"A story for another time, Mother."

Captain began to bark at a red truck that turned into the lane. It pulled into the farmyard; the side door advertising the name "E.Z.J. Brothers & Co. Engraving."

The delivery men helped haul the memorial stone all the way to the site of Granddad's demise. The cantilevered stone trapdoor above the cavern had been dismantled to prevent additional tragedy. Rough-hewn with a polished side, the memorial stone was erected in front of the cavern opening. Engraved on the polished surface were the words:

> Jonah Johann Brandtmeyer:
> Beloved Father and Grandfather
> Here met his untimely rest.
> July 7, 1927 – May 6, 1986
> "I know that he shall rise again
> in the resurrection at the last day."
> –John 11:24

The family stood admiring the memorial stone. Grandma, Noah, and Eleanor were all teary-eyed. Captain rested next to the marker, tongue out, and panting. Reinhardt walked a wide berth around the cavern's opening; something had caught his eye along the trunk of the fallen oak.

"Look!" He held up in both hands what he had found.

"Good eye, Reinster! Now there's a handful of morels!"

SPECIAL THANKS

Thank you to George, Kevin, Johnny, Adi, and Nate for the valuable feedback. Kevin, for the "five minutes" and hours spent reading multiple drafts and editing; George, for the excellent criticism, critique, and editing. Thank you to my wife—all your technical support brought me out from the depths of computer pits and black holes numerous times.

To all my family in Ohio, thank you. Jesse and Mom, thank you for all the support and encouragement. Thank you, Dad, for farming; thank you, Jordan, for making it inspiring and memorable.

C. M. Setledge, 2022

Made in the USA
Middletown, DE
15 October 2022